NEVER HAS A RAIN STORM NOT CLEARED

What is Truth?

You are presented with a choice.
You take it with consequences.
You choose not to take it with consequences.

ROBERT E. BARRERA

The Reading Glass Books
(888) 420-3050
www.readingglassbooks.com
production@readingglassbooks.com

Contents

For my two beautiful children, Bianca and Tom. You guys are the gift that keeps on giving!

Prologue

"November Four One Alpha Delta, you are cleared for take-off," the air traffic control operator stated with a light Southern twang, "After departure, turn left heading three three zero, climb and maintain ten thousand; contact Miami center at one two five point four."

"November Four One Alpha Delta, we're rolling," Tom responded as he keyed the mic.

Tom pushed the throttles steadily forward and kicked the twin 620 horsepower turboprop engines into motion. It was always a thrill how the 11,000-pound aircraft generated the G-forces and pushed him back against his seat. This was his "Living the Dream" magic carpet.

Acceleration was quick, and in less than 800 feet, he was pulling toward him the yolk that controlled flight, and the airplane gently took to the sky, screaming at 120 knots and accelerating with a climb rate of 4,000 feet per minute. Tom loved the thrill of air flight and being the one in control of it; all that adrenaline. He could never get enough of it.

He banked left as instructed and contacted Miami center, the area radar control service, to report he was airborne.

"Miami Center, November Four One Alpha Delta is with you," Tom grinned to himself, happy like a kid on Christmas morning to be among the clouds once again.

"November Four One Alpha Delta, radar contact climb and maintain ten thousand proceed Miami VOR," said the controller.

As Tom finally stabilized his climb and acceleration to 300 miles an hour, he thought about where he presently sat in his life… and how far he'd come.

It seemed it was only a few years ago he was working as a clerk with Federal & company, a purveyor of government services mainly that catered to federal, state, and county agencies. Then, by some stroke of luck (or his charm), one of the agencies suggested he become his own contractor, and they would help him with some contracts. He jumped at the opportunity with the help of several services that helped set him up. Soon, he bid on his own government contract and went into business for himself with a steady income, recognition with the right players in the industry, and the company experience needed to go after the next contract, and the next and the next. Now, he was almost certainly going to be awarded a $20 million credit line to manage the upcoming contract, which looked very promising to be awarded, not to mention the company's current 30 employees and the 30 more he had just brought on. People whose lives and families depended on him and his company. Talk about a lot of pressure. Flying was the best distraction for Tom.

As the twin turboprop stabilized, Tom couldn't help but think of the meeting in Tampa, Florida. After several rounds of negotiations and finagling, he was in the final throes of getting an increase in the bank credit line with the First Financial of Tampa. This would undoubtedly accelerate the start of absolute financial independence. He had worked hard for it. He had eaten a lot of dirt for it. But now, it seemed like all his efforts were coming to fruition.

He was almost 40 with a trophy wife, two beautiful children, and a lovely 4000-square-foot house that boasted a tennis court on an acre in a patrolled neighborhood. No, it wasn't a mansion nor a McMansion, but as a mentor had said to him when he was a boy, "Tommy, you don't want to stand out; stay low key; otherwise, they'll chop your head off." A comfortable house, not too showy, yet quite luxurious by any standard.

He was the youngest of eight, and although his dad had a solid job, spreading income across eight never left much for anyone. Oh, they had plenty of food on the table and got a new pair of shoes each season, but he didn't get the cool toys or the latest bike his rich friends had. What he did have was his big brother showing up at his ball games, his sister helping with his homework, his brothers fixing his flat bike tire, and his older brother helping him get a job at the gas station where he worked. "This is my little brother," was all that needed to be said. At dinner every night, everyone sat around the table. He had family. His rich friends' parents went out to dinner a lot, leaving their children at home with the babysitter. The cool toys… he quickly got over these. Heck, he played with all the games and gadgets his friends got bored with.

At a young age, Tom understood, at a profound level, that family was everything. He had seen tragedy among friends and neighbors; even his own. Tom had seen too many of his wealthy friends all alone with no family support. They were in free fall emotionally and spiritually with only financial backing from their parents… and that just isn't enough. At the end of the day, money could be helpful but by no means was it everything. As he got older, Tom dated a bit but was perpetually unattached, and he wanted more out of life. He married late in order to set himself up as financially independent as possible. Family and living well were the goal, but if he didn't have time for either, then any career accomplishments and personal achievements didn't mean all that much.

Tom dreamed of having the time to enjoy a family. He envisioned sitting on a back porch with his young children before taking them to school. Being home early to be with them before dinner. To put them to bed. That was growing up. Not rushing out of the house a 7 a.m. to some job, only to drag yourself home maybe in time to kiss your children good night. Or worse, to kiss them good night asleep in their beds. Family was everything to Tom; to him, it was all you truly had in the world.

"November four one Alpha delta, after Miami VOR continue to climb to flight level Two Zero, Victor Ninety-seven, La Belle, Victor four-ninety-two, Saint Pete; Tampa; contact Miami center 135.2 good day," chirped in the Miami controller.

"Four One Alpha Delta, roger," Tom replied; he always got a kick from the formal exchange of the aviation world.

He laughed to himself when he remembered the first time he had heard the term "Victor Airways." These were imaginary lines in the sky that went from one VOR to the next. The system gave them names when they created an entire route system, as was Victor 97 from Miami VOR to the Tampa VOR.

Yeah, it was going to be a sweet deal; the bank would create the liquidity Tom needed for different projects in motion and celebrate his financial empire. And all this before he was 40 years old.

It was a beautiful South Florida day with no cloud cover and a light breeze. It made for a smooth and comfortable flight.

During the routine instrument scan, however, he noticed the left engine oil temperature was slightly higher than normal. It is well within the operating range, but not normal is not normal. "I'll need to keep a closer eye on it," he thought.

The rest of the flight was uneventful.

"November Four one Alpha Delta contact Tampa tower 118.3," came in the instructions from the controller.

"Four one Alpha delta, roger."

"Tampa tower November Four One Alpha Delta is with you 5 miles southeast inbound for landing with airport information Foxtrot."

"November Four One alpha delta radar contact, you are number one for landing runway three six," greeted the Tampa control tower. Tom positioned his turboprop nicely on the glide slope to the north- facing runway and began his descent. He approached from the south coming in over Tampa Bay on his continued descent. He looked to his left and saw the spectacular SkyWay Bridge below. So were the joys of flying. You just couldn't get these views anywhere else.

He landed at the Tampa International Airport, and after being directed to the general aviation section where private aircraft were welcomed, he was guided to a parking area and shut down the engines. The greeter picked him up in the golf cart electric vehicle and whisked him to the private terminal.

Here he ordered an Uber. He had thought about the private car but then thought again. He didn't want to be too showy. Perhaps the bank might see him and think he was spending his money, or their money, in a reckless manner. Better look like the bean counter accountant type, carefully watching his expenses. Yeah, that was the best way.

He arrived just a few minutes before the scheduled 10 a.m. appointment and was immediately ushered into the awaiting conference.

He entered the conference room, and to his surprise, along with the consultant-broker, there were several people wearing nametags that Tom did not recognize. These included the bank's chief financial officer, which would be unusual for this type of meeting. Tom recognized him from the bank's annual reports and filings. He had never met nor spoken with him. He could be here to congratulate Tom, but his hackles were up. He was here to close on a loan whose terms had already been negotiated. He only expected his loan officer, Ed Myers.

This was not smelling good.

Rob Peterson, the consultant-broker who had introduced him to this bank years ago and always did the end runs for him, spoke first. "Tom, let me present you with George Anderson, a financial analyst with the Department of the Treasury."

The two men nodded at one another.

Rob continued, "Do you know our chief financial officer, Ephron Kimball?" Rob then extended his hand and pointed to a seat across the table, indicating for Tom to sit.

"Please have a seat, Mr. Bennet, or may I call you Tom," Ed Myers chimed in.

"Tom, please."

"Thank you for the application. We are always pleased to work with progressing businesses. We have had several people review the documents," Myers continued.

"There's been a good amount of activity with the account."

"Yes, we use the credit line for different opportunities, and it's been a great resource for us," Tom responded.

"We see that, Tom. Recently, you seem to have used the line more heavily," Myers looked up from the file he was reading. "Can you tell us a little more about that and what you need the 20 million dollar limit for?"

Tom's warning bells were going off now. This was a file that had been sent over more than 30 days ago, and this guy is asking these basic questions now?! "Um, well, I thought it was clearly outlined in the proposal," Tom said.

"We wanted to hear it from you directly, if you don't mind," Myers said, removing his reading glasses from his nose.

"Well, of course. We are working on a new government proposal, of which we are already very much involved with," Tom said. "If awarded, and we think we have a very good shot at it, we will need these funds to procure the merchandise and inventory to supply the contract."

Something was up, and he could not figure out what it was.

Myers stated," We've been reviewing your financials along with the bank statements, and there seems to be a lot of missing money here…"

After an uncomfortable pause, Tom replied, "I don't know what you're talking about."

"We're not seeing a balancing from the latest funds used from the credit line to an asset nor income that it supports," Myers responded with a little more tension in his voice now.

"I would say you're in a heap of shit," chimed in Ephron Kimball.

Myers looked over to the chief financial officer, then back to Tom. "There is a major discrepancy between the use of the credit line and the assets of your company. It's almost as if funds have evaporated from the company. As if, there has been a theft. Your liabilities are showing greater than your assets," he stated in an accusatory tone.

Kimball went further, "We're not going to approve the credit line. Furthermore, we are calling the existing loan and are going to refer this file to the Department of Justice."

Chapter 1

Tom froze. It was like the shock one might experience for a few minutes after a bomb goes off. Blood seemed to drain from Tom's head, and a cold sweat overcame him. So many implications from one statement— eight words "refer this file to the Department of Justice." The company would collapse, and all those employees and their families would lose so much. The shame. What if he lost his wife and his kids over this? The Feds would start some kind of investigation… and if you start looking for something, you will always find *something*.

The meeting started to break up. Myers got up first and started walking for the exit. On his way out, he dropped an unfolded letter in front of Tom. All Tom caught was a glimpse of the title, "Notice of Default." His eyes could not focus otherwise.

Next, Ephron Kimball, the bank's chief financial officer, stood, looked once again at Tom, shook his head, and walked out.

George Anderson of the Treasury was still writing something on his notepad. As he finished and closed his binder, he looked up at Tom and said, "We'll be in contact." He got up and left without looking back.

Last, was Rob Peterson. Apparently, he was taken by surprise as much as Tom was.

"I am sure I can explain what these people think they are seeing, Rob," Tom stammered.

"I will see what I can dig up and salvage here, Tom. But these people are pissed," Rob sighed, running his fingers through his hair. "I'm not sure what can be done. If they have taken it to this level, they either have something against you or, at the very least, they have made up their minds. I'll call you later. Get back to your office and talk to your finance guy." He walked out.

Tom got up from his seat. He felt like Atlas carrying the weight of the world on his shoulders. Only 30 minutes ago, he was riding on air. Now, he was a pariah.

"Well, no use moping about it now. Pick up the pieces and get the hell out of here. When you get back home, let's see where I stand," he thought to himself.

When Tom arrived at the general aviation side of the airport, he looked over and saw his magic carpet airplane. Someone was walking around it. It should have been all fueled up and waiting for him at the front of the tarmac by now, as he had requested.

Tom went into the office to pay. "Did you fuel up the plane?" he asked. "Yes, Mr. Bennet. We did several hours ago."

"Well, who was just working on the airplane?" Tom asked.

"There should be no one out by your plane, sir. Are you sure he was working on yours?"

"Mine is the only one sitting by itself," he said as he walked over to the window to look at his plane again. Sure enough, there was no one there. Did he imagine it?

"Well, all right, let me take care of the bill and get out of here. Thanks."

He filed his flight plan back to Miami and began the flight check for departure.

Things proceeded normally until he leveled off at 20,000 feet. He trimmed the airplane for a routine flight when he noticed the oil temperature and pressure gauges issue again. The temperature was now a bit higher, and so was the pressure on the left engine.

When he returned, he would need to get that looked at by his mechanic.

That was the last thing he needed now that his finances were unraveling—an expensive maintenance issue on the plane.

Yeah, and what about the plane? It would have to go sooner than later. Shit!

"November Four One Alpha Delta contact Miami approach 127.6," came over the headset speaker. "Four One Alpha Delta, roger," Tom called back.

He tuned in the noted frequency on the radio, keyed the mic, and called out, "Miami approach November Four One Alpha Delta is with you."

"Four One Alpha Delta radar contact continue course one three five degrees descend and maintain ten thousand," came back on his headset.

"Four One Alpha Delta," he answered.

About 35 miles out and 15 minutes to landing, Tom pulled back on the power settings, and suddenly, there was a loud pop. Tom looked to his left, and out the window, he saw smoke coming out of the left engine. An alert started beeping, and red lights began going off all over the panel.

The left engine oil temperature was through the roof, and the oil pressure had dropped to almost zero.

"Shit, shit, shit...!!!"

The plane pulled hard to the left since power had dramatically ceased from the left side, and the right engine was still at full power.

Ingrained emergency procedures kicked in. Tom stomped on the right rudder peddle to turn the plane right and back on course. He feathered the left engine propeller, which basically turned the propeller paddles, so the thinnest edges were facing forward and produced the least resistance to the wind. This made that engine useless, but then again, it already was.

He had practiced the procedure a dozen times, but nothing could prepare him for the actual circumstance. Outside of the power loss and shutdown of an engine, what else was going on beneath the surface? Was there fuel leaking that could cause an explosion? Did the failure take out another vital component? He didn't realize he had broken out in a cold sweat and how tight his hands were gripping the controls. He was scared.

The plane continued on its descent, but faster since it had lost half of its power. Tom stabilized the descent since the plane could operate on one engine perfectly well, though it wasn't ideal.

Tom continued with the left engine shutdown procedure, shutting down the fuel supply and further stabilizing the airplane to hold and fly on a one-sided engine.

"Mayday, mayday, mayday. November Four One Alpha Delta, left engine failure. We are holding on the right engine. Presently stable. Request direct vectors to the airport."

"Four One Alpha Delta, roger. You are cleared priority one for runway nine, right. Turn left heading zero nine zero," he heard on the speakers. "American Two Nine Whiskey abort the landing. We have an emergency with priority for landing. Four One Alpha Delta, you are cleared to land runway nine, right. Emergency vehicles standing by."

"These controller guys are the best!" Tom thought, wiping clumping beads of sweat from his brow.

Thankfully, things continued to hold together with the plane stabilized on the remaining right engine. Tom continued to descend and finally had the runway in sight.

When Tom calculated he was going to make the runway, he leaned over to the right side of the panel and threw down the landing gear latch. He felt the comforting clunk of the gear going down and locking itself in place. Three green lights on the panel confirmed it. At least that worked okay.

As Tom approached the end of the runway, he could see the emergency vehicles on the side with all their lights flashing.

"Welcome to Miami!" Not the welcome Tom had hoped for, but at least he made it in one piece.

Tom engaged a little wing flaps to further slow the aircraft down, but with one engine this proved a little tricky.

When Tom was over the runway still gliding down, with his right hand resting on the twin levers, he pulled back on the throttles and let the airplane gently settle itself onto Terra Firma.

Touch down!

"November Four One Alpha Delta, welcome back. Proceed taxiway Charlie to the general aviation area," Miami tower chimed in.

"Alpha Delta, thanks!" Tom replied with a sigh of relief. He hadn't realized he had held his breathing until he started using his lungs again.

He continued to his parking area. After finally shutting down the operating and life-saver engine, he muttered some gratitude to the engine and tapped his instrument board with a reassuring hand, "Good doggie!"

He sat in his pilot seat for a few minutes to catch his breath and to recall what the hell just happened. You could take it back to the conference room until now, but just the last 15 minutes was enough for a lifetime. Soon enough, he worked himself out of his seat and out of the plane. Dialing his cell phone, he called one of the most important people in the world to an airplane owner—his airplane mechanic, Ernesto.

In this life, you need to know several people intimately. People you can call at three in the morning—a doctor, a lawyer, and a mechanic. If you own a plane, then an airplane mechanic, as well.

It also helps to be a steady source of revenue for them. Tom had observed that when you start any business relationship, be a "buyer" immediately and not a tire kicker. You are put in a special category even if you buy a little. You are a customer. No, a paying customer. They answer the phone when you call.

"Ernesto, Tom here. I have a problem...."

After he explained the details of the flight going out and the excitement coming back, Ernesto came back, "Do not worry, Mister B. I will get on it right away." Yeah, these guys are great too.

After hanging up with Ernesto, another call came through and Tom had to pick up. It was his wife, Ellie May.

"Hi, honey! How was the trip?" She asked, too excited to let Tom get in a word edgewise. "Are we going to the Keys to celebrate with all your new money?" Her question was somewhere between prodding and exploratory. Like, "let's do lunch in Paris," to a possible serious "... for real! We're going??!!" You gotta ask.

Tom's stomach sunk deeper than when his plane's left engine went out. "Noooo, and we need to have a serious conversation later. I am afraid we need to re-arrange some things," Tom cautiously replied (like our entire life and lifestyle, Babe!).

He looked down at his phone for several moments before hanging up and began to walk to his car. Only a few paces in, he noticed two guys walking in his direction. One was dressed on the formal side, and the other was in more casual attire but designed for some manual work.

"Mr. Bennet?" The well-dressed one asked.

"Yes, that's me. What can I do for you?" Tom asked.

"We are with the First Financial of Tampa, and we have papers here to impound your aircraft with call letters November Four One Alpha Delta." The well-dressed man handed some papers to Tom.

The other man began walking toward the plane with a paper in his hand. He then placed a "Confiscated!" Sticker on the main cabin door.

"If you move this aircraft from here, you are in contempt of court and subject to imprisonment. It would be considered theft," the well-dressed repo agent said to Tom, looking him in the eye. He nodded to his companion and then looked back at Tom. "Have a nice rest of your day," he said and walked away.

Chapter 2

A Blurry Premonition in a Café

Tom woke up on the couch in the lobby of his office. It was Saturday morning, so thankfully, no one would show up for 48 hours.

After the fiasco at the airport, he had headed straight to his office to talk to the accountant, Fred Bartholomew, but the man was nowhere to be found.

So, Tom decided to start looking where the bankers had mentioned, in the inventory and accounts receivable section. He combed through the books until late. Ellie May had called several times, wondering when he would be home.

Why had he not seen this before? Was he too busy leading the great executive life to stoop down and go through the grind work of looking at his own books and the state of affairs?

He was broke. No, worse, he owed millions and had no cash in the bank.

It looked like the accountant had embezzled, but proving it from the maze of transactions would be practically impossible. And then, of course, he would have to recover all the monies, that is, if he could prove theft.

He had seen this story before, and he knew how the last chapter ended. Never well for the owner.

Tom headed for home. When he arrived, he sat down with Ellie May, his wife. What a mess. The tears, the accusations, the insults. To Tom, it seemed as if he was only as good as his last cash flow.

He left the house with his stomach in knots. As he was walking to his car, he thought he saw someone in the periphery off to his left. He turned, but there was no one. Was it a tear or just the weight of the whole day combined with exhaustion?

Now, he would have to sleep on a friend's couch for the foreseeable future while Ellie May and the kids would stay with her parents. Tom had no choice but to put the house on the market.

Within a few days, he also had to close down the business and lay off all those employees, since all company funds were seized.

* * *

Phil, Tom's friend with the couch, left for work. Tom, with nowhere to go for the moment, could only stare off into space. He felt paralyzed— he actually had dozens of places he needed to go to clean up dozens of messes.

He sat up and faced the opposite wall and began staring at nothing in particular. For some reason, his focus settled on the light switch. He let his mind start to drift into nothingness. Nothing was pestering him or bombarding his consciousness.

On their own, and without Tom noticing, his eyelids slowly began to close until they finally went all the way down, blocking out all light.

Tom continued to stare, and the events of the past day started floating past his mind's eye. That big screen in your head where you watch your past or future like a movie.

But Tom gently pushed those screenshots past. It was like he was escorting them out of the room until he found himself looking at the light switch. Clear as day. Then he realized, "Hey, my eyes are closed! How can I be seeing this?"

This caused him to jolt back and see all black again... his eyelids were closed. He opened his eyes and there was the light switch exactly as he just saw it.

"What the hell just happened?" Then again, this wasn't the first time this had happened.

It was like he was in another layer. Here, but not as physical Tom.

I must be starting to lose it! he thought. "I better get this show on the road and try to mop up what I can and see what can be salvaged," he said to himself.

It was true, several years before, Tom had started to seek stronger answers. He didn't question his faith or the existence of God, but he did question the authority of the manmade institutions of religion. Were they expressing the whole path? The path that is within us to our spiritual self?

He had gathered with different groups and experimented with various meditations. Many, of course, were shenanigans looking to make a buck selling books or courses. If you are truly "there," you don't need to sell it, nor do you need to justify it to others. You just are.

There were a few sources that truly seemed to point one in the true path. But what is the "true" path, really? Even the master of Christianity when asked, "What is truth?" Remained silent. There are many roads that lead to the same place, and what may be true for one may not be for another, yet it is still a true way.

What was clear in all his studies, exercises, and meditations was that no one can do it for you. Only you can walk your own path. Tom thought of the crude analogy provided by one colorful mentor, "Only you can take your own shit." Doctors can provide laxatives and recommend certain fibers and foods, but in the end, you must do the pushing." How true this is. A difficult and narrow way that can only be achieved by a determined and steadfast individual.

Did he stir something up that was causing all this? He had asked for guidance. He had asked to be given the grace to be in "the space." In the presence of Divinity. He had wondered if his life was more than just earning money, going out to dinner, and making some product or contribution to society.

Did he ask for too much? Were all these catastrophes the result of his illusions of wanting to be a "warrior of the light," as he implied he wanted? It seemed like something... perhaps similar to the photo of the ripped guy with the six-pack in the magazine. You want the look, but going to the gym at 6 a.m. daily is a different story.

He wasn't sure, but he knew he didn't like it. I guess the request to the Divine was, "Hey, I want to be in 'the space,' but I also want to keep my lifestyle, the plane, the bank account..." He was beginning to suspect he may have gotten himself in deeper than he bargained for, if indeed one thing was related to the other.

A little later, after a shower and shave, and a *café con leche* for a wake-up bump, Tom started to call his customers. He had stopped delivering orders as the bank had seized all inventory at his warehouse, but maybe some part of this could be turned around.

The first call was to his point of contact at the Federal General Services which managed and had issued several contracts still ongoing.

"Lieutenant Sanders, good morning. Tom Bennet with the Bennet Company. How are you this morning?"

"Very well, Mr. Bennet. What can I do for you?" Responded Lieutenant Sanders.

"Well, I am having some difficulties and I wanted to alert you. I have had a disagreement with my bank that funds the inventory I deliver to you. I am afraid I will not have the scheduled shipment for this coming week."

Silence.

"Well, Mr. Bennet, when can we expect it?" Said the Lieutenant after a pregnant pause.

"Ah, well, that's just it. I am not sure as my operation has been shut down, and I need to regroup, perhaps using someone else's facilities. Is that alright?"

"Mr. Bennet, if we do not have the scheduled supplies by end of next week, you will be in breach of contract. These are critical supplies, and you were offered this very lucrative contract on the basis of your timely delivery. If the supplies are not delivered as promised, we will probably cancel the remaining term of the contract and sue you and Bennet Company for specific performance."

Tom was taken aback by the abruptness. "I will try to make it happen one way or another," he finally said.

"Is there anything else?" The lieutenant asked in a cordial manner now that he had a potential deadbeat on the other end of the line.

"No, Lieutenant. You have been most helpful," Tom said and disengaged the line.

Prick! Well, that wasn't actually fair. Lieutenant Sanders had pulled for him, and he was probably instrumental in being awarded the contract. Now Tom's failure looked bad on Sanders. *Yeah, I get it.* Tom thought. *It's his ass on the sling as well as mine. Sorry, Lieutenant.*

Tom went out to get breakfast at a little Cuban café where you can get a Cuban coffee and tostada— Cuban bread buttered and toasted—for less than $3. That was his speed and budget at the moment.

After he had sat at a table and ordered, he looked around the restaurant and spotted a nice-looking girl of about 25 sitting at a nearby table having her breakfast. But something struck him in that moment, and he couldn't stop staring. She was very attractive, but it wasn't that. It was something else.

Then, like a zoom lens, his eyes targeted her abdomen area and everything looked kind of dark and fuzzy in that area. Like a shadow and a little blurry. Tom started to feel a bit queasy.

He couldn't help himself any longer and did the unthinkable; he got up and walked over to the girl. "Excuse me. I am sorry to interrupt your breakfast, but I am having a kind of funny feeling, and I think you should have your stomach area checked out as soon as possible."

"What?!" She blurted out, astonished. *Is this guy trying to pick me up, or what?* She thought to herself while staring at Tom.

"I know," Tom said, "I sound like some kind of lunatic, and I promise I am not stalking you, but I was compelled to come over and say something. Please, humor me, although you have no reason to do so, and go see a doctor as soon as possible."

The woman sat there, speechless. She looked somewhere on the spectrum between angry and embarrassed.

Lastly, Tom pleaded, "Could you call me and let me know if I am crazy?" He handed her his card with a sheepish smile. "I am a happily married man with two beautiful children, so don't worry."

He walked away and left the rest of his breakfast. He couldn't eat. He was shaking, not believing he just did that.

Chapter 3

A Dark Spot Tempts Eve in the Garden of Herbology

Eve Peroni lived in a small, cozy apartment with high ceilings and big windows in the mid-town area of Miami. Not the new fancy part, but what we could call old Miami. The bay wasn't visible from her place, but the water was a short walk from her home.

Eve was passionate about being outdoors and loved gardening and growing things. So, it was no surprise to her family when she chose herbology as her final educational path. Eve dedicated herself to the study of plants and their medicinal properties.

The history of herbs, their healing powers, and their many uses is as old as recorded civilization. Modern medicine still derives its drugs from this knowledge and the actual herbs themselves. Balancing the different tannins, flavonoids, and alkaloids can produce miracle remedies.

She had finished her studies in herbology at a boutique school in the northeast dedicated solely to the research and training for the use of herbs, and she was well-trained. She hesitated to call herself an expert. I mean, who could? Her interests were on the wellness side, not the cooking with herbs side. Some called this holistic medicine, and she didn't go that far.

She opened a small shop in the trendy Buena Vista area where old meets new and was lucky enough to snag a wormhole of a space on NE 2nd Avenue at a workable price. Herbs are not something that fly off the shelf, nor are they a high-margin product, but if one is looking for medicinal remedies to ailments, they know where to look. Eve was not in it for the money, as much as the satisfaction of improving lives. Of course, cash flow is always important when you need to pay rent and buy raw materials.

The herb environment helped her connect with her other interest. Specifically, Eve was very interested in the art, if one could call it that, of connecting with her inner self. It was actually more than an interest and she actively meditated and was intrigued with magik. Not the charlatan-type tricks, but the real connection to the other layer of the Universe, of Life itself.

Her interest in the occult was more than a fascination. Years earlier, she had had several unpleasant experiences, for lack of a better word, with unseen forces.

The Universe attracts and repels as your Will creates.

It was not a surprise when a good-looking guy walked into Eve's shop one Tuesday morning looking like a train wreck. Yeah, this guy was definitely in need of something… I mean, short of cyanide. He had a desperate and stressed look, yet something else caught her eye.

"Can I help you?" She asked.

Tom looked up from several bags of herbs he was eyeing on a shelf as if someone caught him by surprise. "Oh, no. Well, actually, yes. I am not really myself lately, and I am looking for something. I am a little rattled. You know, stressed and I need to sleep at night. I am hesitant to take the stuff at the local pharmacy and a friend suggested I come by here." Indeed, Tom had, just this past week ran into an old college friend, Ted. As they were catching up, the conversation sidetracked to Ted's wife, who had a bout with some digestion problems the doctors could not figure out. He had mentioned Eve's herb store by name as the place where they got positive results.

"Good choice from your friend," she smiled. "These herbs may not work as fast, but they are… natural. The body understands. Let me see what we have." She turned and went to the back of the store.

She returned with a few items in her hand, "Are you looking for something to restart or improve your sex life, or something else?"

She said it so matter of fact that Tom didn't know how to respond. No man wants to hear someone challenging his libido. Geeezzz! "Ahh, well, um, nothing like that for the moment."

Eve chuckled, "I'm sorry, I am not trying to be nosey nor rude or impertinent, but we want to find the ingredients that will bring you back to where you want to be."

Just then, as she looked back up at him, the light from the window caught Tom at a particular angle as he was turning. She noticed a distinct glow around Tom's upper body. Just below the glow, however, was a darkening.

She was no expert by any means, nor some enlightened person, but this meant something. She was just not sure what it was. The fact that a novice like her was even seeing it meant that the energy was very strong. Should she point this out to this customer or let it ride?

"You can try a mixture of rosemary, myrtle, and marjoram for a soaking bath. Lemon verbena and chamomile for tea with a little ashwagandha. I have a little horsetail for an energy pickup in a tea to help with relaxation."

"Uh, thank you. I'll try the tea. I don't think I will be doing the bath soaking, though. Not, at least, where I am staying at the moment," Tom said, shaking his head.

"Okay, let me ring this up. Will that be cash or charge?"

"Cash."

Eve's head was pounding. *Should I say something? This guy is going to think I am hitting on him, but I can't just let this go…*

As she was rounding up the sale, she said, "Um, if you are interested in herbs and natural wellness, I and some girlfriends that care about this are getting together later tonight. Would you like to come by?"

"Oh, no thanks. That's very nice of you, but I am not really up for socializing. If you know what I mean." He was turning to leave when Eve lightly touched his arm to hold him back.

"Actually, there is a bit more. I don't know how to explain it, but I am sensing something about you. No, around you, and I want my friends to look at it. I am not that good at this, and they may have a better feel."

"I don't understand. What are you talking about?"

Clearly frustrated by her own pussy-footing on the topic, she blurted out, "There's some shit hovering over your upper body that's jumping out at me. I am not sure if it is good or bad. If you're curious and have nothing better to do, please come by!"

"Ohhhkaaaay, then…" Tom lightly chuckled at the forwardness of this attractive girl. "I can come by."

"Great," she gave him the address, which was nearby, and he turned to leave.

As he was walking out, she noticed the darkness again. It seemed to have gotten much larger.

Chapter 4

The Dark Side of a Guided Meditation

Later that evening, Tom headed out to meet with the lady from the herb shop. He found her attractive, but not in the *Vogue* magazine, upscale fashion sense. No, this girl, well, woman, actually, had handsome features about her. Classical lines, an excellent upright posture, and a confidence about her that she was not only comfortable in her skin but knew who she was. The whole package made her quite appealing. The kind of attraction that when she walked into a room, everyone noticed her. The thick brunette and hazel eyes didn't hurt the overall package either; he smiled to himself.

Tom had taken his tea when he got home. He rested a bit answered some emails he had sent out earlier to probe some possibilities.

He headed out to the get together with the herb shop lady.

Heck, he didn't even know her name. She invited him, but not to be *with* her. Was she being altruistic? Did she want to help him just for the sake of it? Tom was not familiar with this type of person. All his working career it was always, "What's in it for me?" He wasn't used to offers with no strings attached.

He arrived at the address the lady gave him, but he wasn't sure if it was correct. It was not what he expected. Heck, he didn't know what he was expecting, but this was a little house in the same Buena Vista neighborhood on one of the side streets in old Miami, with all its charm... and it was not it.

Perhaps he thought she was inviting him to some public meeting hall. This could prove to be more exciting, a private affair. Intriguing even.

As street parking was a little difficult in this neighborhood, he parked a few blocks away and walked back to the house.

As he made his way up the entrance pathway, he noticed someone coming toward him from the opposite direction on the sidewalk. It was already approaching dusk, so he didn't see the face, but as the person approached with a positive step and a nice figure, it became clearer. It was the shop girl.

"You were able to make it!" She said with a friendly smile. "I am sure you will get something out of this."

"I'm...looking forward to it," he replied. "By the way, I took some of your herbal tea. Sad to say, nothing happened."

Eve stared at him, her mouth a little open as if to say, *Are you an idiot?* "It is a subtle approach. It needs to build up in your system and counter your stress. Just because it's natural doesn't mean it is not powerful."

"Fair enough," he said with a slight shrug.

"If you want powerful, you can take something like Bella Donna. Your heart will stop in about five minutes," she turned and walked up to the door.

Ouch! he thought, *She's got a bite and is a little feisty... I kinda like it.*

Eve lightly tapped on the door, turned the doorknob, and opened it as she walked in. Clearly a part of the family here. "Hey, everyone, it's me. I brought company," she called out.

Two women were in the living room area immediately to the right of the foyer. One was about Eve's age and the other a few decades older. The older one was slightly overweight and had a motherly aura to her. The kind of woman who wouldn't get hysterical if her child was drowning in the pond. She would just reach in, yank him out by the collar, place him on dry land, then continue having her conversation with her friend. This woman looked as if not much could phase her.

The other lady had an earthy nature about her. Nothing particular about her wardrobe or look. It was just the first thing that came to Tom's mind.

"Hi darling!" The older woman chimed in with a cheery, welcoming tone. "Who's your friend?"

"Ah, this here is..." she turned to Tom, "I'm sorry, I did not catch your name. My apologies. I'm Eve. And you are...?"

"I'm Tom Bennet," he said, looking from Eve to the ladies, "We met at Eve's store this afternoon, and she invited me over this evening."

"Well, welcome, Tom Bennet. Please come in and have a seat. Orlando is making some tea and should be out shortly. I'm Cheryl, and this is Anita," she said, pointing to the earthy woman.

"Cheryl, when Tom was at the shop this afternoon, I caught a glimpse of something over him. I got a strange feeling. Not good, not bad, but I thought maybe..."

"Sure, let's settle in, relax and see what comes out," Cheryl added over the noise of the clinking of dishes and silverware and shuffling of cupboards coming from the kitchen.

A few moments later, a good-looking guy Tom guessed was in his mid-thirties, emerged pushing a trolley with full tea service. There was a teapot, cups and saucers and all the accessories, and a three-tiered plate with cookies and pastries.

"Wow, that looks fantastic!" Tom said.

"Hello, I'm Orlando. My pleasure, and welcome," he piped in, "I was overhearing a little of the conversation in the kitchen, but I didn't catch it all. When these ladies aren't being slavedrivers, I work the room, as they say. I have a little bakery shop nearby for my day job."

"Oh, Orlando, stop it. If you didn't make the best baked goods in the county, we wouldn't bother you," Cheryl said, and they all laughed. "Orlando has a sense about him that helps us in our gatherings. So, when he says, 'works the room', he is being very kind. He can 'move' the room, actually," she added, looking over to Anita and Eve for affirmation. They all nodded in agreement.

This a tight group here, thought Tom. They had a genuine comradery, which was not always easy to find or to have.

Orlando served everyone, and they had their tea and goodies and chatted about nothing in particular. It did not escape Tom that they never gossiped about anyone. The conversation focused more on events, cultural shifts, and personal experiences. This energy set the tone of the group and who they were. It was refreshing.

Tom felt relaxed and at home here. This crew had a formidable ability to create a calm and welcoming atmosphere. It was the most excellent thing he could remember in a long time.

There was a pause in the conversation, and Cheryl turned to Tom and said, "You have a Don, a gift. It surrounds your presence. An energy. You need to develop it if you want to use it."

Tom held his breath for a moment, like he was waiting for her to continue...or for the other shoe to drop.

"However, I also sense the darkness. I am not sure what to make of it, but I sense it will interfere with any progress you wish to make. It will challenge you. If I am reading this rightly, it is up to you and your Will to overcome this darkness and prevail."

When she finished the room remained quiet for a few moments. Orlando then chimed in with, "I think she is stressing that you may have opened up something. I'm getting a bit of that too. You will need to move forward or back off." He cautiously inserted, then let it sink in.

After a silent pause, Anita, the earthy woman, spoke up, "Tom, would you be open to doing a little meditation with us tonight?"

"I am not sure I know how, but yes, I will try," Tom cautiously replied, not knowing what he was getting himself into. "I have delved into this before, but I don't think with much success…" *and certainly not with the results I am living with now,* he thought to himself.

"That's okay," she replied. "People get very intimidated by meditation, but it is simply being totally focused on something. I am sure you have done this before but may not have realized it."

Tom looked at her, puzzled.

"I'll put it this way," Anita continued. "Have you ever been so focused on something so much that you don't even hear when someone talks? They finally shout, 'Did you hear what I just said?'… and you didn't?"

"Yeaaaah," Tom said with a starry look in his eyes, as if he was catching on. "I get that way on my computer when I am intensely working on a project."

"Well, then you already tasted it. You just have to get yourself in that spot," Anita reassured him. "The hardest thing to show someone is an experience they have never had. How can you describe the taste of chocolate to someone who never had it?"

After a slight pause, she continued, "Let's try something. Okay?"

"I'm in," Tom added; he was open to just about anything at this point.

"Great…" she smiled. Everyone in the room let out a silent breath. There was communal relief that Tom was a willing participant in his own evolution. His energy presence had captivated the group. Some call it an aura, but that is for those who actually see the energy; make no mistake, a person's energy can be felt. You often see it when someone walks into a room. It's not that they are good-looking, tall, short, how they dress, or their posture, but somehow, they command attention without even speaking. This presence is their energy that is so strong it's exuding out.

Anita started, "Close your eyes, Tom and try to relax. I know it seems impossible, and your mind is racing in a million directions. Look at that big

TV screen in your mind and watch. Watch the thoughts coming across, but don't run away with them. Observe them."

Tom's eyes were closed, and he became keenly aware of the sound of air inhaling and exhaling through his nose and mouth.

"They may come from your right-hand side," Anita continued. "Escort the thoughts through to your left- hand side and out. Like you're seating the thoughts in an auditorium. Let them pass along."

Tom shifted a little in his seat but remained silent.

"Keep the focus on the thoughts coming through," Anita said softly. "If you accidentally keep traveling away with one of these thoughts, like remembering that event in the park or at the office, don't chide yourself. Gently come back to the observation. After a while, this bombarding of random thoughts will subside," she continued.

The room settled into silence as everyone participated in the exercise.

"Ambient noises, like cars in the distance, birds and such, might appear a distraction, but actually they help you stay in the present. Just don't hop into one of the cars for a ride." As Anita spoke, Tom could hear the smile on her face.

The evening had already settled in, and the lamps in the room were already mostly off or on low. There was some subtle lighting in the breakfront and several oil paintings illuminating the room in a soft atmosphere.

They were quiet for about a half hour when Anita softly broke the silence and said, "Let's get a feel for what I mean by 'being present'. Let's take a journey."

Tom was ready to go wherever this woman led.

She began, "Visualize you are on the beach. It's a very nice and wide beach with white powdery sand. You hear the surf in the distance because you are not at the water's edge. You are at the far edge away from the water where there is a copse of palm trees that provide a canopy from the bright sun. You are in the shade. You are seated, cross-legged, and looking at the beach.

"You are watching yourself from behind on your big TV screen in your mind. Do you see yourself? You are looking at yourself from the back in that big TV screen in your head. Now move closer to yourself. A little closer. Closer still. Slip into your body and feel the cool sand under your legs. You are in a bathing suit, so your legs are exposed to the sand. Feel the gentle breeze from the ocean. It brushes across your exposed chest and face, even moving your hair.

"You are present. The moment you think, 'Oh, this is so cool,' you lost it. You are no longer present; you are looking back at yourself, but you are no longer in yourself. Experience this all at the same time. Try to hold it as long as possible. Not observing it, but being it. Being in this moment." She became silent.

Tom was moving with the experience Anita was creating. He indeed saw the thoughts coming across and passed them along as she said to do. He slipped several times and realized he was someplace else. But, as he was guided, he did not berate himself. He simply returned to the observation. Eventually, things started to become less hectic. Like his mind was becoming tired of trying to fool him. He saw every image Anita described clearly—the water, the long sandy beach, the copse of trees, himself on the sand. This was the most real he had felt in a while. He felt so alive.

He entered his body when Anita had walked him in, and he could feel all of himself at once. It was kind of eerie, yet exciting and incredible. Placing his mind in this focus, he could feel the bottom of his thighs on the cool sand, his chest receiving the breeze, his hair gently tossed by the breeze, his arms, his toes... all of himself at the same time. It was exhilarating!

He touched on being present, fully himself for this moment.

He felt he was able to hold the moment for longer. Of course, by observing that he was holding the moment, he was no longer in the moment.

As he was, once again, in that copse, he "felt" the air around him change. It wasn't the breeze. No, it was something else, like when your vision ripples looking at something on a really hot day over an asphalt road or in a desert. More than that, however, it did not feel good.

It was beginning to feel sinister. The whole scene, moments earlier, the epidemy of tranquil, was now shifting... and he couldn't place it.

The pressure continued to build, and he didn't know how to reverse it. Or could he? After all, he was here more as an observer.

Then, suddenly, he felt a rush coming from under him. It was like a void. Like being swallowed. It was nothingness, and through his entire being crept a sensation of aloneness. A loneliness so profound he had never been exposed to. The most horrible sense of being. The void, a darkness, kept coming at him so fast he felt the opposite sensation, like he was falling. Out of nowhere, a hideous face rushed up from some depth. He could not fathom where it came from. It rushed right toward his face and was huge and snarling with a large hooked nose, warts, and huge black eyes. "Ahh," Tom moaned as his head shot backward, hitting the bookcase behind him. "What the hell was that?!" He gasped and began breathing hard.

"Whoa," he was breathing hard.

Everyone had immediately come out of their trance, and Eve and Anita came to Tom's side. Anita took his hand and began rubbing his arm in a gentle, warm motion.

Eve started moving his head away from the bookcase and looked for damage. She heard the bump quite loudly and checked to see if he was bleeding.

"What happened, Tom? What did you see?" Asked Cheryl. Everyone, of course, was looking at him, also curious.

Tom explained everything, then asked, "What was it? What the hell just happened?"

The three girls and Orlando all looked at each other with something left unsaid.

Chapter 5

The People Vs. The Bennet Company

Sydney Markowitz was the only son of David and Rose Markowitz. He had graduated from the University of Florida law school, and after several unsuccessful interviews with the larger Florida law firms, he was offered a position with the U.S. District Attorney's office for the Southern District, covering activities in the Miami area and neighboring counties.

His father, David, was very proud of Sydney for following in his footsteps. David had been in private and public law throughout his career and presently worked with the Department of Transportation in their legal department. He didn't consider himself a bureaucrat, but he enjoyed the law more than the rat race of the law. "Making the numbers" and making questionable decisions in the name of "billable hours" was not how he wanted to spend his time.

Sydney wanted a little more than his dad, however, and was anxious to make a name for himself at the U.S. District office. So, when he received a complaint from the First Financial of Tampa bank on potential irregularities with the Bennet Company, he jumped on the opportunity. After all, successful businessmen usually cut corners which is how they probably become successful, he reasoned.

He was determined to use this as his vehicle to propel his career.

Sydney opened a file on the Bennet Company and began to compose a profile to eventually be brought to a grand jury for an indictment, followed by a full-scale, high-publicity trial to make an example out of Tom and his company for conducting bad business practices.

Chapter 6

Coffee with a Side of Voodoo

Tom left the house kind of spooked. After a round of goodbyes, he started walking down the entryway. After only a few paces, Eve darted out the front door after him.

"I'm sorry if you had an unpleasant experience," Eve called out to intercept Tom before he left. "Everyone was a little taken aback by what happened. We are not used to seeing something as…," she paused, "… powerful and abrupt. Are you sure you weren't a witch doctor in your previous life?"

Eve asked the question in such a mocking but sincere manner that Tom just stared at her. The two of them then shared a laugh, and the tension was broken.

"I guess I will have to bring out all my voodoo dolls from my closet and remove all the pins," Tom finally said.

"Seriously, I feel a little responsible," Eve replied. "But, this just strengthens my feeling that there is something else there. As Cheryl said, you have a Don, a gift, and it seems like it wants to come out."

"I don't know," Tom said with a contemplative sigh.

"If you would like, we can go get a coffee or something and unwind this. That is…if you want?" Eve asked.

That was the best offer Tom had received in quite a while. A beautiful, intelligent woman offering to take him out. *I'm getting a little full of myself*, Tom thought. He didn't mind that she had an intriguing spiritual component to her.

"Yeah, let's go. I would like that," Tom said with a half-smile.

"Let me get my handbag and say my goodbyes to the gang. Give me a few minutes," Eve replied before turning and walking back into the house. In short order, she was back. "There is a little hole in the wall up the street, but it's clean, and we can talk in there. I think there is sidewalk seating, and it's a nice enough evening."

She took control of Tom's arm, and they walked the few blocks talking about nothing in particular, which helped distract Tom.

Eve described their destination as a "little café." Once they arrived, Tom realized it was a little more than that. It was an eclectic shop with African art and Santeria accessories like a *"mal de ojo"*, an evil eye that wards off evil. Oh, and there was also a counter to order coffee, tea, or wine.

Tom ordered two glasses of chilled white wine and joined his "date" at an outside table. It was a quiet evening, with only one other couple at a nearby table. The girl was a bit too loud in that Tom could hear her "whispering". They had to be on a first date because she was expounding on how sincere and caring a person she was. Tom found this to be commendable until the waitress came by and asked if everything was okay.

The girl didn't even look up but spat out, "... the wine was not chilled as I asked, and where is the extra bread?"

The waitress blushed and apologized and then took back the wine. Tom turned to Eve. "Can you believe that? The girl is melting butter with her 'sincerity' but then bites the waitress's head off and treats her like dirt for something so inconsequential. Either she is incredibly self-serving, or she has so many layers of ego she doesn't know which role to play."

Eve looked over to Tom reflecting, "That's an interesting observation, Tom," she replied. "What do you mean by 'layers of ego?'"

"On one level," he began, "I sometimes envision life as someone sitting in an empty theater with the lights out. Only the stage is lit. You are the only one in the audience, and there is a play in progress. In the play there are several actors presently on stage, and you are one of them. The You in the audience observing is your soul, the real you. The character you play on stage can be useful, but many of us get carried away with it and become the character. We lose sight of the real You, or me. The one sitting in the audience."

"Wow, that's a fascinating way to put it. I don't think I have ever heard it looked at in that way, but it's kind of refreshing when you think about it. It uncomplicates the view. How to look at life and all its inconsistencies," Eve reflected.

"This girl seems to be so entrenched in whatever character role she thinks she needs to be that she has forgotten who she is and that the waitress is a person just like her. A person with aspirations and feelings, sadness and joy in her life, with the need to be validated and loved... like all of us."

"That is a beautiful acknowledgment," Eve smiled.

"I'm no genius, Eve, nor have I invented anything. Didn't Shakespeare say, '... life is but a poor player that struts and frets his hour upon the stage and then is heard no more...'? A little cynical view, no doubt, as I think we do a little more than that. We can certainly do miracles, and many do. We all have the power and ability within us. Not the same ones; not everyone can be a neurosurgeon, but you do what your Don, as you guys said, can do."

"Very true," Eve nodded.

"If you wipe away all the ego layer shit blocking you from seeing the You sitting in that auditorium seat, you will know your gift, and you will freely act on it," Tom added. He was a little worked up, somewhere between the girl at the other table and the evening in general. He continued in a lower voice, "And if that little gold digger next to us wasn't so concentrated on nailing this guy, she might actually prove to be a nice girl."

"Well, don't hold back on us, Tom Bennet," Eve, wide-eyed, said with a grin. She couldn't help but laugh quietly. "Tell us how you really feel."

Tom chuckled to himself. "Sorry, I get a little carried away sometimes. I'm talking too much. Let's talk about you, Eve. Tell me a little about yourself."

She had been so concentrated on Tom that she had been leaning over on the table, so she sat back in her chair.

"I'll tell you what. I have to go. I am not avoiding the question or trying to be mysterious. Heck, you already know a lot about me. I am a herbologist, have that little shop, and hang out with crazy friends. That's enough from one night. But let's get together again. This week if you would like. I am interested to see why that thing jumped out at you back at the house. Then we can talk some more. Okay?"

"Uh, sounds good. This was…nice. Thanks." As he waved his hand at the casual setting they were in.

A few moments later, the check was paid and Tom left a nice tip for the frazzled and abused (by the other table) waitress. Tom and Eve got up and then stepped to cross the street through a space between parked cars with Eve ahead of Tom.

Tom felt a tingling in his chest, like that feeling when you jump into freezing water. He wasn't sure why he did it, but his hand shot out and grabbed Eve before she reached the other side of the parked car on the street. He felt a premonition; something dangerous was about to happen.

Suddenly, a motorcycle shot past way too quickly and way too close to the parked cars. Eve looked at Tom and back to where the motorcycle had just passed, nearly hitting her. She then looked back at Tom, her eyes like saucers. "Did you see that motorcycle coming or did you sense it?"

"I…I sensed it. A flash of something in my mind's eye—I think."

"We definitely need to talk further. No joke now."

Chapter 7

Cheryl and the Occult

Cheryl was intrigued by her recent guest, Tom.

She had delved into this realm several times since her first experiences as a young teenager. One night, shortly after the death of her grandmother, she awoke in her room and sensed an unnatural feeling of quiet and stillness. Exceptionally so. She felt a presence in the room, although she could not place where. Then, she felt something rub her left foot.

She gasped... and dared to look up from her covers and saw the shadow. The room was devoid of sound, and her entire being was focused on this darkness within the shadows of her room, stroking her left foot.

The shadow perked up when Cheryl's gaze fell upon it. It stiffened, and she was terrified it would attack her. Except it did the opposite. It turned sideways, like a playing card, completely flat and thin on the side, and zipped out through the seam of the closed door of her room.

The experience changed the path of her life. She pursued a life in academia and finished with a Ph.D. in religious studies. She never let go of the non-academia side of it and pursued her own inquiries into the occult world.

It is not difficult to find people intrigued in the occult. With Ouija boards at a party and occult themes making it into TV, film, and books, there was never a lack of a captive audience. What is more difficult to find, she eventually realized, were serious, conscientious, and respectful people to explore these mysteries. She had found these qualities with the intimate group, the one Tom had just visited with.

They had all experienced what she would label "advanced perceptions." A feeling or intuition that was then or later confirmed to be true. An insight or clarity. Even a premonition.

During meditation sessions, they all experienced a sense of other beings participating. Some were helpful, but others... well, let's say you wanted to run in the opposite direction. They had to be careful as they had all experienced a sense of foreboding, a darkness that appeared to be watching them from the edges. They were careful with how they conducted their sessions. Cheryl's academic studies of ancient tomes brought much light into their studies... and what previous experts cautioned and guided.

The visitor Eve brought tonight was something else entirely. She had not seen energy like this before. It was powerful, yet somewhat scattered and uncontrolled. But the most intriguing thing was that it seemed to disrupt the darkness.

Eve's new friend had something she could not put her hand on, but it could prove to be explosive. She had to get Eve to bring him back over again. They needed to review this again.

Cheryl didn't deal with the darkness; on the contrary, she was a warrior for the light. But in that realm, the darkness was always in the periphery. You always knew it was present, but quietly on the sidelines, perhaps waiting to be invited, if you were so inclined.

Where there is light, there is always darkness. Where there is cold, there is heat, and so is the makeup of the Universe.

Last night, however, she noticed a quietness in the periphery—something she had never experienced before.

Who was this Tom Bennet? Was he stirring up the forces of evil? Was he awakening it? Could he control it?

There was a time she had stirred this up herself, and it did not go well. She would have to warn Eve.

No, wait. Even better, she would ask Eve to bring him back.

Chapter 8

An Unexpected Tango with the IRS

Tom woke a little after 5 a.m.

He had to pick up the kids at their mother's house and take them to school. If Tom wanted to be part of his kids' lives, this was one of the ways to make it happen. It may not have been the traditional Ozzie and Harriet of doing things, but you take it where you can get it.

Before leaving that morning, Tom pushed himself to do an exercise routine. He hated to exercise, but there was no doubt it made him feel better, and one of his fears in life was getting old in terrible shape. It wasn't the getting old part that bothered him; it was the getting old with your body falling apart. "*Hecho tierra*," as the Cubans say, meaning reduced to dirt.

So, Tom did a little something every morning. Ten minutes, that was all. He felt like if he did an hour in the gym, he would never go back again. He would always have the excuse that he didn't have an hour to spare that day. But 10 minutes? Even procrastinating, Tom couldn't talk himself out of it.

Tom took his kids to school every morning and picked them up in the afternoon, often shuttling them to their after-school athletics as well. Call him Mr. Mom, but this was how he got to spend quality time with his kids and exchange with them.

Growing up is not just about feeding and caring for your children. It is a daily interaction. The silly comments, the offshoot thoughts or deeds. It is a question, "Jane said this to me today ..." This allows you to provide guidance and reinforce their strengths and what's important. Even "what does such and such mean?" Can allow you to be there for them. At least, that's how Tom felt about it.

Tom's unemployment, or what he liked to refer to as, "new self-employment," allowed Tom to have an open schedule. How ironic. He had wanted to watch his kids grow up and be there for them and with them... but from a millionaire's position. Now he was doing it but from a pauper's position. But at least he was doing it. Crazy.

That morning, when Tom picked up the kids, he handed them the bag lunches he made for them. In these lean times, school lunch money was not one of his options. Fortunately, they liked Tom's lunches.

"What's in the bag?" Bailey, Tom's son, asked.

"Well, there's a BLT, and I made some sugar cookies. I also loaded a small baggy of corn chips from the big bag, and I have a can of mango juice," Tom replied, looking back at Bailey strapped in with his seat belt.

Bailey nodded with approval and a smile. Lunches could be fun.

After Tom dropped them off, he headed to a small Cuban café where he was to meet a friend, Armando, who was trying to set him up with an opportunity to get back on his feet again. Even though these little eateries, which were all over town, offered an inexpensive breakfast of café con leche, eggs, and tostada, Armando was paying. *That's even a better deal*, Tom smiled to himself.

Tom arrived a little after Armando, and as he entered, he could see his friend waving from a table. Tom made his way over to sit down. As he did so, he was greeted by a friendly face. "*Hola, mijo,*" Rosa smiled. She had been working here forever, but today she had a worried look on her face.

"Que pasa, Rosa?" Tom asked, inquiring in Spanish and with the look on his face about what seemed to be troubling her.

"Eduardo, my son, did not get the driver job," she sighed.

"Tell him to try the Goya distribution center in Doral. I think they are looking," Tom smiled as she nodded gratefully. He then weaved his way toward Armando and offered the man a warm, traditional Latin hug.

"Tom, something is coming up on a state contract," Armando offered right away. "I think it might fit your bill. It's a logistic thing. They have the trucks and what they need is the service people—no equipment expense on your part. Only labor and you can get with the state employment agency, Workforce Florida, to provide the talent. Hell, they'll even make payroll for you for the first six months. And since you have virtually no overhead, you probably can outbid anyone who shows up." As he finished, he smiled to himself and took a sip of his café con leche.

Tom didn't speak; he was having a hard time believing what he was hearing. Was this too good to be true?

"Well, what do you think?" Armando said as he looked up.

"I think, yes," Tom said with a big grin. "I think. Thank you very much, Armando. You certainly pulled my titties out of the fire with this one."

Armando threw his head back and chuckled. The man then provided all the details on the upcoming contract and where to file it. "I think I can even help with the presentation as I have the outline already done. Let me work on it and get back with you later," Armando offered.

After brainstorming a bit more and finishing breakfast, Armando left first after paying for both of them. They agreed to meet later so Armando could help Tom with the bid paperwork.

As Tom exited the cafe, he noticed a man standing to his left. He wasn't a vagrant, nor was he likely to be asking for money or a handout, but this wasn't the next vice president of Merrill Lynch either. The man was in Tom's path to his car. As Tom walked past him, the man spoke in a low voice, just enough for Tom to hear him, "You have opened something that has called attention to yourself. Stay alert."

The mystery man was not looking at Tom, but if he didn't know better, he would say the man was just speaking out to the world or at least talking to himself. Somehow, Tom knew this message was for him.

As Tom turned to say something, a car honked. "Tom!" a woman's voice called out.

Tom looked, and it was Angela, his old secretary. As Tom looked back, the mystery man had moved further away, and only his back was visible—and Angela was waiting.

Probably some greeting or gossip anyway, since the office closed, but she was an invaluable assistant and always had her ear to the ground. Tom made his way over to Angela, "How are you, darling? You are looking good."

"Oh, Mr. Tom, as good as can be expected. I am on my way to a job interview. None of these people are bosses like you were. What a drag this is. How are you holding up?" she asked with a genuine look of concern.

"Well, I might have a bit of good news. Armando just turned me on to an opportunity. If it comes through, I will call you back. I can't ask you to hold for me but stay loose if you can. You know we work great together," Tom said, leaning on the window of her car.

"Well, count me in. Let me know how it goes. I've got to run to that interview now, and the traffic is horrendous. Don't forget me! Pleeeezz," she said as she pulled out of the parking lot.

Tom straightened up and looked around to see if he could catch his philosophical mystery man when his cell phone rang.

"Is this Thomas Bennet?" The caller announced.

"The same," Tom replied.

"This is revenue agent Anderson from the Internal Revenue Service. I was calling to give you a heads-up. After review of your company's audit we started six months ago, we have disclaimed the aircraft expenses for the past five years. We feel you could have taken commercial services. The reversal tallies up to $129,642 you wrote off. Since we add it back in, you should have paid taxes on that income. Calculating taxes due five years ago and with penalties and interest for five years, you have an obligation to the IRS for $152,486. We will be sending this notice out this week."

After he hung up with the agent, all Tom heard was a ringing in his ears; he felt the blood drain from his head. He was lightheaded and reached over to the nearest parked car for balance.

When it rains, it certainly does pour!

Chapter 9

Rosa the Café Waitress

Rosa Martinez had immigrated from Cuba some years back. A small window of opportunity to emigrate from the Caribbean Island nation opened every once in a while, and when it did, she jumped at it. She first had to go out through Spain and from there, was able to come to the United States, a country she had dreamed about for years.

She was able to come with her husband Paco, a nickname akin to Frank, and her infant son Pedro.

She was grateful and even more so when she got a job at La Tacita Restaurant. It's a cute name for a little hit of Cuban coffee, "the little cup," but it also had a full menu for breakfast, lunch, and dinner.

Rose worked mostly the breakfast and lunch shifts which she liked because she could pick up young Pedro at school by three in the afternoon.

That was then. Pedro was a young adult now.

Rosa had been raised Catholic, although while in Cuba that was not allowed. However, she believed deeply in her faith and that there was a higher power greater than her and all creation that looked over her and protected her.

Lately, however, it seemed she was blocked. She could not think clearly, and Father Ramirez at her local church did not seem helpful or all that concerned.

It was like the church was a gatekeeper to God, and she needed their permission to talk to God and get His help.

"Why is that?" She thought to herself. On one hand, the church said the kingdom of God is within you, but on the other, it seemed one needed to seek permission or the approval and the guidance of a priest.

Her son, Pedro, had graduated high school and was looking for a job while attending junior college.

He was being offered something with a group out of Miami Beach that dealt with luxury cars and high-end tourists. Pedro was enthralled, as any young person would be, with all the money and wealth, but Rosa knew better. This influence was not a healthy environment for an impressionable youth.

She didn't know what to do. It was like a cloud was covering her head. That morning, she saw that Tom Bennet customer who she always liked. He was always so uplifting, even without saying a word, although he always had something nice to say. Even just his smile was comforting. His presence brought a certain energy about him. She couldn't explain it, but the whole room just felt more at ease. Calm. That was it.

Then, Tom casually mentioned the jobs available at the local Goya distribution company. Good pay, daylight hours of work that could work with Pedro's school schedule, and a solid company.

The direction suddenly became very clear for her and for her Pedro. It was like a cloudy sky opened a patch for her to fly through.

She liked that guy, Tom. He was definitely something special.

Chapter 10

A Messenger from the Universe

That evening, Tom needed a break, so he went down to the shore to look out and try to unwind. The steady and reliable drone of the ocean waves rolling onto themselves ratcheted down his nerves a few notches.

It seemed like every time he poked his little head above water, some giant scythe came by to chop it off.

On one hand, a tremendous opportunity with Armando came up, not that he had it yet, and on the other hand, he got an ominous call from the IRS. The IRS problem was not an "if" but a "when." Jeeeezz.

He is crying in his own soup feeling sorry for himself a little while sitting on a park bench overlooking the surf with the full moon rising off the shoreline horizon. Just as he put his face in his hands, a man came from behind and sat on the bench beside him.

"For godsakes, man," Tom thought to himself, "of all the benches on this empty beach, you need to sit on this one?"

"The crystalline waters of a lake are blurred by only a slight breeze that ripples the waves," the stranger rattled off as if he were speaking to someone other than Tom. "But as soon as the breeze stops and the waves cease you can see 100 feet to the bottom. The layers within oneself are very thin, if only we can calm them down for just a bit. Then we will see the depth of our being."

Tom was looking out on the surf listening to his new neighbor. He couldn't put his finger on it, but whatever the man was saying sounded almost like a prayer. His voice was soothing and felt profound.

After all the weird things occurring in Tom's life as of late, why not this too? Some random guy appearing out of nowhere to unpack the mysteries of life. Tom had always felt the mysteries of life were always around us, waiting to be discovered, if we only looked.

Finally, Tom said while still looking out at the surf, "Those are pretty words, but they are hard to put into action when the whole world is crumbling on top of you."

"If you were God," the man began, "and you had all of creation to use to deliver a message, how would you do it?"

Tom knew a rhetorical question when he heard one, so he let the man continue.

"Say, you want to be a doctor. What good would it do for God to present you with an opening for a doctor position at the local hospital if you presently have no training, no experience, and are not a doctor? Wouldn't it be better to show you where you can start your training? Perhaps, have you look right instead of left when you are on the bus so you can see the bus bench ad offering you to train as a medical technician and with financial aid at no cost?"

Tom took in the man's words and didn't feel the need to interject; the new arrival was making some sense.

"But, *nooo*, that's just a coincidence, you might say," the man continued. "So, you bump into an old friend at the supermarket, and she tells you of this great new opportunity that trained her and placed her in a hospital job paid for by the hospital. But your head is still in the sand. Then one night, your car gets a flat tire in the rain. Your spare tire is flatter because you forgot to repair it the last time you had a flat. You see a light on a house at the end of the street and you walk there and ring the bell. The owner answers and lets you in to use the phone to call for service. As you wait for the tow truck, you realize she is the head of enrollment at the local college for medical studies. The Divine

Universe gives us as many chances as we need, but we must be alert. Everything that befalls us is with purpose. Nothing is by chance, and all for our betterment. You get a flat tire in the rain, and you curse the bad luck. But is it?"

"Why are you telling me this?" Tom finally asked the stranger.

"You are on a path, whether you realize it or not, seeking further depth into yourself," the stranger replied. "Open your eyes to what is presented to you daily, not as a torment nor a bad event, but as an answer or even guidance. If you don't get the job you were applying for, perhaps it's because it was not in your best interest in the long run. Perhaps, it's because *you* asked for something better, but you are applying to this because it is available and convenient. Accept what is presented in this light. But don't confuse a negative answer given to you as a sign to give in or give up. Don't consign it to fate either. Life is full of challenges for you to complete for your own spiritual enrichment and maturity. 'No', may just mean you need to try harder. When you can't hire a gardener to cut your lawn and have to do it yourself, it may be so you can know landscaping. It may be to prepare you for something in the future that requires this knowledge. Sort of like the medical training to later become a doctor. Don't shun what appears to be misfortune."

"Who are you?" Tom finally asked, shaking his head.

"I am a messenger. We will talk again." And with that, he got up and left as mysteriously as he arrived.

Chapter 11

The Cost of a Smile

The next morning after dropping his kids off at school, Tom headed for Armando's to continue working on the proposal and pricing the items required to put the deal to work.

"Can I bring you some breakfast or something for an early lunch?" he asked Armando on his cell phone.

"Yeah, that would be good. I rushed out of the house this morning and didn't have time for anything. You can pick something up at the supermarket. Thanks," Armando replied.

Tom was passing a local market as he hung up, so he quickly hit the brakes and turned abruptly, the guy behind him nearly slamming into his rear bumper. Of course, the guy behind him laid on his horn.

"Serves him right," Tom thought while shaking his head. "Following so close. Damn, all I could see in my rear-view mirror was the guy's windshield. Not the hood, not the front grill, not any kind of separation. Where do these people learn to drive, and where do they learn about reasonable spacing between cars?" He thought. "Heck, who signed off on that guy's driver's license?" He was shaking his head.

He navigated through the parking spaces, parked his car, and headed for the supermarket entrance.

As he walked in, he headed for the prepared food section and picked up a small variety of items to create a breakfast for him and Armando.

As he headed for the checkout, Tom's cell phone rang. "Bennet," he answered without looking at the caller ID.

"Mr. Bennet, this is Calvin Rosenthal with the Department of Justice, Southern District." "What the hell?" thought Tom. He stopped walking and planted his feet in the middle of the supermarket aisle, concentrating entirely on his left ear where the phone was. "Yes?" Tom answered.

"It has come to our attention of some possible discrepancies in your former company, Bennet Company, with a credit line," Rosenthal said, not even bothering to exchange pleasantries. "The line was held by a federally insured institution, which brings the issue to this office. We are opening an inquiry for a criminal investigation, and this call is to alert you that you are a target."

Tom sighed, shifted his feet, and ran his fingers through his hair. After some silence, Rosenthal returned,

"Are you still with me?"

"Yes," was all Tom had the energy to say.

"Well then, I will note in the file you have been alerted. Have a nice day," and he hung up.

"A nice day, jerk-off?" Tom thought to himself, "Where do these people come from, babbling cliches so disproportionate to the message?"

Listless, he traipsed toward the cashier checkout, his thoughts scattered. None of the places or possibilities good. When the government gets involved, they will look until they find something. It seems a government employee will need to justify why they spent so much time on your file, so they have to find something... anything.

He was distracted with his own misery, but when the checkout line inched forward and he looked up, he couldn't help but notice the sadness on the checkout girl's, otherwise, pretty face. The customers weren't interested in the slightest, nor acknowledged her existence except to claim their groceries.

When it was finally Tom's turn, he looked at the cashier's nametag, which said "Katie" and then looked her in the eyes with a smile and said, "Good morning, Katie! And how are you today?"

Katie looked up a little surprised because no one usually spoke to her. "Good morning. I'm okay, I guess." Her eyes told a different story.

"Well, you look rather dapper for just being okay, Katie," Tom said, trying to cheer her up. "You're like a little sunshine on this dreary morning." He finished with a smile.

He noticed the girl crack the slightest smile. That was enough for Tom; he changed her mood. She handed him his breakfast, looked up at him, and said, "Thank you, and you have a nice rest of your day." With, now, a nice simile.

Tom smiled again and nodded. "Thanks! You just made it nice!" It always surprised him how big an impact one can cause with so little effort. Not that he was congratulating himself or anything. This exchange with the cashier and cheering her up a bit may be only in his head, but what the heck? What did it cost? He actually cheered himself up!

As he left the counter, he overheard the lady behind him greet Katie with a cheerful, "Good morning!"

Yeah, courtesy *is* contagious, but sincerity is moving…

He walked out of the market and was looking out for his car. Did he leave it on the right side or the left? Out of the corner of his eye, he noticed some movement. He looked over, but there was nothing there. Did he just see a shadow?

Perplexed, he finally spotted his car and headed to Armando's.

Chapter 12

The Butterfly Effect of a Good Deed

Katie Atkins was the seventh child of a loving and united family. Her father worked at the local hospital in the lab and her mother had been a stay-at-home mom for as long as she could. But the operation of a seven-member family became too much for the Atkins budget, and Mom had to get a part-time job to help with the family expenses when Katie was too young to be independent.

She had her siblings, of course, but as the youngest, she was usually left behind as everyone was occupied with their busy lives. Sports, after-school activities, boyfriends, girlfriends, and all that entails growing up.

By the time Katie was involved in her own adventures with after-school activities her brothers and sisters were already much older and past this stage of life. She was by herself, again, with only her school friends to associate with.

It's not that she was an orphan, but people need acknowledgment, and everyone wants to be recognized for their accomplishments. Most importantly, by one's family and parents.

So, scoring the goal, being voted team captain, or winning an academic excellence award in science became kind of hollow for Katie without the affirmation of her family.

When her lacrosse teammates made a goal or had a great run down the field, many had their mom or dad or both on the sidelines. Katie had neither. For no other reason than her siblings were older and somewhere else, and her mom and dad were at work.

So, it was no surprise when she met Justin, who looked at her as something special. He was handsome enough and was involved in his own activities at school, although he was no star. No, he was not captain of the football team nor school student council president, but he had a quality that beat all those. He paid attention to Katie and listened when she spoke. When he was able, Justin was her cheerleader on the sidelines and her escort on her way home. They talked about everything, including their future together. Justin was adept with machines and how they worked. He helped his father tinker with the family car and with light repairs. He was eager to finish school and get out into the workforce.

Although it appealed to Katie to leave her family home and start a life with Justin after her schooling, she was not so sure about starting out so unprepared.

She wanted to be something more. Somewhere she felt she could contribute and be part of something bigger. She was not sure what it could be, and all the jumble and pressures around her were clouding her focus.

Do this, go here, you have to do this, you have to do that. That's what other people wanted for her. But what did she want? What was the best for her?

That morning at her cashier job at the market, a strange thing happened. Some gentlemen came up to the register to purchase some items and he looked at her straight in the eyes.

No one does that. People looked at her like another shopping cart or an ATM needing to process their purchase. But this man did something different. He looked at Katie as a person. He acknowledged she existed… and actually wished her a nice day. Not a hollow comment like when people say, "let's do lunch," or, "how ya doin'," when they could not care less about either. No, it was a subtle shift, but you could see he actually meant what he said. He waited for her response.

Katie thought about this for the rest of the day. It opened up her mind and started to bring new clarity to the path she needed to take in her life.

If someone could make her feel this important with a simple smile and acknowledgment, perhaps she could do the same for others.

The direction she was looking for was opening up. Like a cloudy sky starting to clear. She didn't know exactly what she wanted yet, but she knew she needed to do more for herself. Self-development. Definitely pursue a career. Whether it was in the medical field or cryptology using her math skills, she didn't know yet.

Justin and their life would have to wait.

She thought about the nice man at the cashier aisles. Did he realize how big of an impact his seemingly small and brief effort had on her? She sent a little thank you prayer his way.

Chapter 13

One Step Forward, Two Steps Back

When he arrived, Armando informed Tom he had completed the final touches to the presentation they had worked on. He could submit it today. The government agency was in a bind for this, and they had already called to ask when he was submitting the proposal.

"The sooner, the better, Tom. You have a good shot because you're local, and it's not a big enough proposal to interest a big operation," Armando informed. "You might want to start lining up drivers and speak with an insurance agency just in case you get the award. The government is ready to move right away when they award this."

They emailed the finalized proposal to the government procurement officer in charge. Now it was a matter of waiting.

They had their little breakfast, and after thanking his friend, Tom headed off.

Tom decided to head over to Eve's shop across town to get a little more of that tea… at least that was the lie he was telling himself. What he really wanted was to see her again… let's call a spade a spade.

Ellie May was still his wife, but he needed a friend. A sounding board, and that was not something available to him in his marriage.

He headed toward the Buena Vista area where the shop was located. As he approached the mid-town area, the traffic became impossible.

He realized the issue was some kind of rally taking place up ahead blocking traffic. He figured he would pull over and park wherever he could and walk the rest of the way. It was a nice day, and walking and pacing had always been a mechanism for how he solved problems.

He finally found a spot, parked, and began walking. He saw that his route to Eve's would take him right past the rally, so he decided to mosey on by and see what it was about.

There were about 100 people of all ethnic origins, so this wasn't a racial issue. He moved in closer. The speaker at the improvised dais had a portable microphone with a speaker.

"… and those high taxes are the cause of all your misery and why it is hard to get a job," the speaker roared, "… we need to stop paying the taxes…" he continued.

"Right on, brother," Tom shouted out. The speaker, a tall Black man with a beard that was a little unkempt, saw Tom as he shouted and was revived by the audience's participation. He waved to Tom to come up, hoping for support to help keep his momentum going.

Tom figured to himself, "what the heck," and moved up to the dais with the speaker as he was handed the mic.

"Yeah, I can't agree more with my friend here," Tom pointed to the speaker, "after all, what the hell does this government do for us except take our money?" He shouted.

Many in the crowd nodded in agreement.

Tom saw a somewhat disheveled man in the audience wearing a cast on his arm. "You, sir," he pointed to the man with the cast, "you fixed yourself up by yourself I see," pointing to his own arm to signal the man's cast.

The man looked down at his arm, a little confused, and called back, "No, they did this at the Jackson Memorial Hospital free clinic," not quite understanding where Tom was going with this.

"Oh, my mistake, then," Tom said and pointed to a mother with her infant, "... and you miss, did the government take something from you? Your job? Child's education, perhaps?"

The young mother replied kind of indignant, "My child goes to public school," she responded, like saying "huh, take that," until she realized the public school was paid for by the government and she was on the receiving end. Her look was not so indignant as it began to dawn on her.

"How about these terrible police, huh?" Continued Tom as he waved his arm in a wide sweep showing the several policemen casting a big circle protecting the crowd in the event of any violence. An ambulance even showed up to help anyone in distress from the big gathering.

The crowd scanned the area and began to look at themselves with a little embarrassment. Maybe they had been picking the wrong fight. The government and bureaucrats like police, fire, and schoolteachers were not their enemies.

When the crowd realized the hypocrisy they were proposing, they began to break up. The speaker was incensed that Tom had ruined his show, and his false narrative was revealed as a sham.

He grabbed back his mic, and with a scowl, said, "What you want to do that for, man? I had them eating from my hand."

"Perhaps, because you had them eating trash, my friend," Tom retorted. "Feed them hope and reliance on their own abilities, and you may get farther." He turned to make his way toward Eve's shop.

As he was walking away, one of the policemen approached him. Tom thought, "Oh no, not now," but the policeman said, "we noticed how you disrupted the angry crowd and wanted to thank you. I'm Lieutenant Ames with the Miami Police Department. Here is my card if you ever need something from our side," he said as he handed his card to Tom.

"Well, thanks. It wasn't my original intention, but that speaker was riling up the crowd with a bad message, and I hate that," Tom replied.

"Perhaps we can call on you again sometime," officer Ames said with a sincere smile, "Please reach out to me. We would love to have people like you on our team. After all, our job is to help the community, not kill them," he smirked.

Tom shot a look back at the dispersing crowd. It was an instant, but it seemed like there was a dark haze over the remnants of the group. Then, in a disformed way, it just as quickly evaporated. It was strange, though, like a fog that didn't want to leave. It all happened in fractions of a second, but it was unmistakable.

"Thanks, Lieutenant. I may surprise you and call upon you when you least expect," he grinned. "Sometimes a simple mango can alert you of a problem," and he continued on his way.

Tom thought to himself, "Did I just say that? What was I thinking? I am starting to babble…"

The lieutenant watched Tom walk away. He also was a bit confused by Tom's last statement. He shook his head not trying to read too much into it, and turned back to his work with the dissipating crowd.

Tom's cell phone rang, and as he already had it in his hand, he pressed the answer button on the first ring.

"Bennet," he answered.

"Mr. Bennet, this is procurement officer Roy Anderson with the department of transportation," said the caller. "I am looking at your proposal submitted for some logistics and drivers."

Tom held his breath, "Yes, sir?"

"We want to award this to you," Anderson continued, "but several things have come up within the department, and we would like to make a few adjustments to how the initial request is structured. Can you come by later today to discuss this?"

"Where? When?" Thought Tom, his heart thumping out of his chest. In his most calm and collected voice, he said, "Of course, Mr. Anderson. When would it be convenient? I can make myself available."

"If you can make it late this afternoon at our offices, that would be great as we're a little pressed for this. I believe you have our address as it is the same one on the proposal."

"That would be fine. I can be there at, say, 4 or 4:30 this afternoon?" Tom said.

"I'll see you then, Mr. Bennet, and thank you for the prompt response to this." Anderson hung up.

As Tom was reflecting on his good fortune and wanting to call his friend Armando to thank him, he heard the sound of a crunch somewhere behind him. He turned around to see a garbage truck backing into the side of his car as the side window broke into a thousand pieces, the sun catching the sparkles of the glass fragments.

He had just dropped the collision insurance on his car last week to save money. "Good move, Tom," he thought to himself as he was shaking his head.

Chapter 14

On the "Eve" of Something Great

In spite of all that just happened, Tom decided to continue with his original mission and go see Eve at her shop.

So, after he finished with the police giving the garbage truck a ticket and getting all the insurance information, he headed for Eve's.

For the moment, she seemed to be the only soothing ointment in his life. At least, from the short time he had spent with her the previous night at the café.

It's not that he had given up on his marriage, but it seemed his marriage had given up on him. Could it be that love ran out when the money ran out? He didn't want to be so cynical, but the reality was staring him in the face. When the chips were down, Ellie May ran for cover instead of hanging closer… that was how he was reading it, anyway.

When Tom arrived, Eve was crouched in the front vitrine of the store, trying to place some new display. She was in the most awkward position placing her new collection when she looked up and saw Tom standing in front of her on the other side of the glass window on the sidewalk. She grinned.

He winked. "Top of the morning to ya," Tom said as he walked into the store, a little bell clanging from the door announcing a new potential customer had entered.

Eve twisted in her present position to face him, "good morning to you. I didn't think I would see you again after the other night. I would have thought you would have been halfway through Texas by now," she said. Of course, she did not mean it. She *so* wanted to see this Tom character again.

"No, I'm not that easily spooked, thank you very much," Tom said with a warm smile.

She laughed as she wormed her way off the display. She was secretly delighted to see this mysterious caller, but at the same time, she needed to maintain her composure and dignity. She couldn't very well just flounder over him. Some sort of posturing was undoubtedly in order… or so her grandmother had taught her. "Well, it's nice to see you survived the other night. What brings you back around?" She asked.

"I was out of the tea recommendation," he said.

Ahh, Eve thought, *Let me throw this guy a lifeline…* "Of course," she said, "how did that preparation work for you? Did it calm you as you wanted, or do you need something stronger? What tickles your fancy, as they say?" she asked and grinned at him.

"I'm not sure," Tom replied. "I actually came by to see if I could invite you to lunch."

"Umm, if you could give me five minutes, I think we could sneak out for a quick bite. Is that okay?" Eve asked.

"Yeah, that would be perfect," he said.

They walked out of the store a few minutes later after Eve locked up and placed a "Be back in 15 minutes" sign on the front door—a classic great escape for a small business.

As they were walking to the café up the street, a guy parking his new model Mercedes sports car looked over to Eve and called out, "Hey babe, when you want a real man look me up," referring, of course, to Tom.

Without skipping a beat, Eve turned to him and said, "He doesn't need a car to measure his dick size, asshole. Get a life." As casually as that, she continued walking with Tom.

Tom was completely taken aback by this otherwise damsel-in-distress character, or so he had thought.

"That's quite a mouth on you, darling," he snickered as they walked past the Mercedes heckler.

"He's just a frustrated traveler confused as to what he is or what he wants," she said. "I'm not here to show him. That's not my job, and, quite frankly, I don't have the time or the patience for people like that."

They settled for a little shop with an open-air counter facing the street. These typical cafes served *croquetas*, croquettes to English-only-speaking Americans, which are ground ham or chicken mixed with a bechamel sauce and spices. Then they are formed into little torpedoes, breaded, and lightly fried for a crisp outside and soft and flavorful inside. Quick and delicious.

"You were pretty quick with your retort back there, I must say," Tom started in.

"When you get pushed, you need to push back, Tom. Otherwise, all of life just runs all over you. It's not that one cannot be tender and compassionate, but throughout all of nature, there are roses with thorns. We can't let the thorns dissuade us from enjoying the rose. Don't you think?" She looked at him with such an innocent expression. "Nevertheless, you don't need to get pinched by the thorns either."

"Of course, you're right. It's just that right now, so many sides are hitting me at once; it's as if there is a concerted effort to take me down. Does that sound crazy?" Tom asked with a kind of pleading in his eyes. "It's almost like I did something to piss some important guy off, and he is sending his goons after me. I'm not sure where or how to push back."

"Maybe we could have another session with Cheryl and Anita. They always seem to see something we may not see ourselves. I know I feel something when I am around you," and after she said this, she got that expression like she said too much. "I mean in an energy sense…" she quickly added.

"Yes, Eve," Tom grinned, "I understood where you were coming from, although, let me throw in, I do enjoy the company." He was smiling as he finished.

"I don't know, Tom; I have read about people who awaken certain malevolent energies. Were you involved in any seances or activities to call on the dead or things like that? Even as a gag at a party?" She asked, half in jest but paying close attention to Tom's response.

"No, at least not that I am aware of."

"Well, you could not help but be aware of a session like the other night unless you were unconscious," she blurted out with a "duh" expression on her face. "History is replete with people awakening dark forces. Maybe you accidentally kicked a rock that ended up being a hornet's nest. Ouch!"

They both laughed a little at Eve's slight gallows humor.

"Do you want to meet later?" She asked. "I can clear it with the girls."

"I have this important meeting across town later this afternoon, but then I can come by. Call me and let me know if we're on or not."

"Okay, will do" she leaned back to take in the sidewalk traffic. "If you need to go, don't worry. I'll take care of the check," she added.

"Well, you're full of surprises today. First, you castrate the asshole in the Mercedes and take me to lunch. What's next?" Tom raised his eyebrows and smiled with a *Well?* Expression.

"Don't underestimate the man on the street Tom. Guys think they're the only ones who can kick ass and take names. Sometimes, the best man for the job… is, well, a woman." She was staring at him with a sincere, yet confident look.

"I am seeing this live," added Tom, grinning, "... and I will happily accept your invitation because, heck, things are tight, my car was just smashed in, and who can refuse an invite from a beautiful girl?" He was laying on the charm now.

She grinned, "Yeah, well, you don't get those invites from beauties often." She was now laughing. "I'll call you later to confirm the evening. Good luck with your meeting."

Chapter 15

Finding Warmth in the Unknown

"… and what does the great Tom Bennet, industrialist extraordinaire, sought after by governments and capitalists alike, have to say for us tonight?" She taunted him as he was finding a seat in the small, cozy library.

"Ah, Maggie, stop it. I'm just an ordinary guy trying to make a living," he said with a *c'mon… puh-leezz* expression.

Tom's thoughts drifted back several years to a party he attended. Maggie Johnson was the hostess and the wife of a successful investment banker in town. They enjoyed a comfortable but not ostentatious home in the trendy Pinecrest area where each property enjoyed one plus acres along with a spacious interior.

This home accommodated a quaint but cozy side room, which Maggie had creatively turned into a kind of library slash study. It was more of a getaway from the hustle and bustle and general commotion that went on in her house. Some would call it a "man cave," but she used it more than Ben, her husband.

She was catching her breath from the day's preparation as the party was moving into full swing when Tom entered the room for the same reason.

Maggie and Tom were old friends from the circuit and just living in the area, going on forever, so the barbs were neither new nor offensive.

"Well, that's not what I am hearing," Maggie came back as he had seated himself on the high-back green leather chair, complete with brass upholstery tacks. "I heard from my real estate office you now operate your own fleet of trucks out of your own warehouse." She had an expression of mock astonishment on her face.

"Don't believe everything you hear, love. Yes, my name is on the title, as well as on the large mortgage note. The bank is the real owner. I'm just paying the bills," Tom said, smiling back.

"Awe, Tommy, what's bugging you? You look perplexed for someone who should be dancing the jig?! Why you have that beautiful and fun, Ellie May, your two kids… well, I could eat them right up, your beautiful home, and a thriving business." Her hands and arms slightly opening as if making a presentation of fine furnishings.

It didn't escape Tom that she was a successful residential realtor of high-end properties in her own right. She was a hell of a saleswoman. But he also knew she had a master's degree in theoretical mathematics. She had been swooped up after graduating by a government agency she did not talk much about and had worked with them for several years until she met her Ben. Tom wasn't quite sure, since Maggie did not talk about this, but he thought she was disillusioned with the direction the government was taking her studies. She never did anything with it after hooking up with Ben.

He looked over at her for a long moment.

"Is this all there is to it? A party in a nice house, restaurants, a vacation every once in a while, buy a newer car?" He said it with an expression of someone who reached the end of a puzzle game only to find out the "mystery" was some bogus find. Something almost worthless.

She settled back in her couch and looked at him. It was an "I wasn't expecting that" reaction on her face. Her demeanor and whole expression changed. Maggie was always a profound thinker with her feet firmly on the ground. This was one of the main reasons Tom had always liked her and her husband loved her. She was an essential sounding board and always easy to talk to.

She looked out the French windows into the ongoing party for a moment as she composed her thoughts. "Wow," she simply said, still looking out at the party as if she was talking to herself. She turned her head and looked straight into Tom's eyes. He had been staring at her waiting for a response or some reaction.

"No, that's not all," she began. She contemplated some more. "You have something," she paused, "… more… we all have something more."

She was feeling her way around the topic, then continued. It felt like there was some reluctance in her voice, but it was more a difficulty in expressing something in words that have no words to define it. Like when you want to express a dream.

"It's so easy to get lost with all the stimulus we have around us. I'm talking from birth. We have to reach into ourselves and identify who we are. What I mean is, at one point we separate our body from ourselves. We even say, 'my body feels good, or bad, etc., implying your body is one of your possessions, like a car, or a piece of furniture.'" She paused, "But it's definitely not you or us. You understand this at some level of consciousness."

"I think I am getting what you're saying, but where does one even start? I guess I feel like I have been looking, but half the battle is just defining the path to get there, so you know how to approach it," Tom cautiously contributed. "Don't you just want to scream out to this Divine entity, 'Hey, just tell it to me straight, will ya'! Stop with all the code and secret meanings,' " he said with exasperation.

"Except, if you and your angel are in such different dimensions, communicating like you are seeking to do, it may not be possible. What if a being from another galaxy landed on Earth? Not from Mars, which is in our solar system, but, like somewhere really, really, else?" She eyed him for effect. "Why, we may not even recognize the being was even present. They could be so advanced our carbon-based flesh and blood could be beyond them. How would they communicate with us? How would we with them? How would we even know they were here?" Her eyebrows went up. "Well," she continued, "maybe they could shift some molecules within us to cause our bodies to 'feel' something, perhaps through magnetism or a flash of a color in our mind's eye," she said. "We could go on and on, but I think you get where I'm coming from." She was now staring at Tom.

"We need to look elsewhere from our physical environment. Or, at the very least, observe more of our environment," he said as he tilted his head to the right with a questioning look.

"Darling, did you get another case of the white wine?" Ben poked his head in the doorway. "Sorry if I'm interrupting," he said as he saw Tom in the other chair.

"No trouble. We were solving the world's problems," she smiled back. "Yes, there is an unopened case in the pantry. I'll be out shortly."

"Sit tight," Ben said, "I can take care of that, but do join us soon. Guests are asking for the hostess," he said with a caring smile.

"We'll be in shortly, darling. Thanks," and she blew him a kiss. She was so grateful for such an attentive and caring partner... and she didn't take him for granted.

She looked over to Tom. "Close your eyes, take a few deep breaths and focus on one thought that you want to ask for. Just one, and don't let it be superficial, like a new car. But, at the same time, don't make it unattainable."

At that moment, when Maggie directed Tom to close his eyes, there was a wash of warmth that came over him. Almost like a father's hand on one's shoulder showing encouragement and the unspoken words, "I am with you." It would be difficult to explain in words, but a sensation of belonging came over him, and from the depth of his being, he asked, not in words that scrolled through his head, but as a feeling, a thought, like when you see a tree and know it is a tree. The word "tree" doesn't pop into your head, you just know it. "Show me the way. Give me guidance and strength to be in your space." All sound evaporated, and although Tom was in the darkness of a world with closed eyelids, he didn't feel alone.

It seemed like Tom was in this moment for a long time when he felt a gentle warmth on his hand. He opened his eyes, and Maggie's hand was over his. She was looking at him intently.

"Let's go back to the party."

They both knew there was nothing further that needed to be said.

Chapter 16

The Perils and Pitfalls of Offering Help

"What happened to the car?" Isabella asked as she got in. Tom had been right on time getting her from school, even with the traffic and the caved-in car.

"A garbage truck backed into it. Fortunately, I was not in the car," Tom said with a smile and a light sigh.

"Wait till Bailey sees it. You know how he loves adventures and stories," she was wide-eyed, examining the broken glass and caved-in door on the passenger side behind the driver.

"Whooaaa! What happened?!" They both heard from a distance as Bailey approached.

Yep, everyone loves a good story, thought Tom. He was just not that in the mood to get into it. "Okay, you guys, I need to drop you off immediately and get to an appointment. I hope you don't need me to take you anywhere."

"No, that's cool, Dad," Isabella pitched in. "I have homework." "Me too," added Bailey.

"Great," said Tom. "We'll hang out tomorrow, then. How was school? Anything new?"

They chatted and exchanged stories on the drive home. Tom always loved this time with his kids. *Here is where you get to know your kids and what they are thinking*, he thought to himself, *and depending on your response, how you influence them*. Kids are sponges; they don't miss a beat. As Eve put it earlier, "don't underestimate." Just because they're little doesn't mean they're small.

They came to a traffic light and there was a guy at the head of the line with the obligatory sign stating "any help please" on it.

Tom looked at his demeanor and clothing and condition in general and shook his head.

"Aren't you going to give him something?" Bailey asked.

"He's got a pair of Nikes on. Those shoes are nicer than mine, Bailey," Tom said, looking at his son. "This guy has no business being here asking for money." He wanted to add, "he's fit and strong and can easily find a job anywhere."

Things like this bothered Tom on some level. He wasn't clear which one, though. He thought about the complexity of human nature. One of the most treacherous journeys you can engage in is helping others. On so many levels, they *may* resent you, and all you are doing is being concerned and helping, usually financially, but often with just a physical hand. Not everyone, of course, and not in every situation, but it's there, and you usually don't see it.

The recipient may accept your dollars with a smiling face, and the funds will actually have served their purpose, but deep down, they resent you. Is it because you are presently wealthier than they are and can offer the funds? Or because you have a better job situation? Who knows the underlying cause, but it's there. And they may be secretly thrilled if you have a downfall.

As he thought again, the human psyche is very complex. Of course, this didn't apply to this alleged vagrant, who definitely was not, but the thought lingered until the light turned green, and he scooted forward grateful and happy with his fabulous kids in his car. Even though he was presently unemployed, he chuckled to himself.

Chapter 17

A Little Sunshine Peaking In

Later that afternoon, Tom met up with Lieutenant Roy Anderson with the Florida State Department of Transportation field services, who was arranging the logistics contract Tom was bidding for.

"Good afternoon, Mr. Anderson," Tom stretched his hand to greet the man as he entered the sparsely decorated government office.

"Good afternoon, Mr. Bennet, and thank you for coming so quickly. As you know, this need came upon us rather quickly, and we appreciate your interest and prompt response," Anderson replied. "I know you read the Request for Proposal and bid accordingly, but there has been a new update, and I want to see if you might be able to accommodate the situation."

"If I can help, I will do what I can," Tom said.

"The deal originally involved manning the state's truck fleet with your personnel," said Anderson.

Tom nodded.

"However, now, the state's risk management department feels the liability to the State may be too great if non-State employees are driving the trucks. We want to propose an alternative if you agree," Anderson said while shuffling a few papers on his desk. "The State will lease our trucks for one dollar to you or your company. You will operate them with your licensed people and insure the vehicles. Then you will use these trucks to fulfill the logistics contract, which includes hauling parts and equipment for this department all over the State."

Anderson looked as if he was trying to maintain composure, but Tom could tell was pleading for him to accept. Trying not to play his hand too hard, Tom pretended to be thinking, consider the change as if he were being put out. However, he wasn't going to milk it as this change screamed opportunity, so Tom responded, "I think we can do this Mr. Anderson. Your advantage to deal with a small company is where we can be flexible. I will ask that we adjust our bid proposal to include our cost for insuring the fleet. This was not a consideration when the State managed the fleet."

"Of course, that is not a problem. Can we work this out now and get the paperwork completed this afternoon? You could then start preparing for your first orders... perhaps by next week?" Anderson gave off a pleading look which Tom knew meant that the man was in a bind.

"Let me call my insurance guy and see if I could get a quote, and then, of course, I am at your disposal," Tom said. He then stepped out of the office and tried his friend Jim Baker who had handled his office insurance, as well as home, airplane, well, all of it. Baker was a problem solver.

After greeting Jenny, Baker's longtime assistant and receptionist, she put Tom right through.

"Wow! Isn't this a pleasant surprise? Tom Bennet in the flesh," Baker jubilantly answered. "I am sorry to hear about all your... how can I put it, adventures, Tom. You know if there was something I could do all you had to do was call."

"Well, as a matter of fact, you can," Tom replied.

"Shoot."

Tom explained the whole State deal and the new twist with the trucks and him having to insure.

"That's very doable, Tom, but we need all the vehicles' inspection numbers. You know, their IDs, and we are going to need to go out there and take some photos of each truck and assess if they have any damage. The insurance carriers don't want to insure something that's already damaged and later have to pay for it," Baker explained.

"Hmmm, these folks are a little pressed for time, Jim. Can you give me a rough estimate on the cost to insure the fleet of 23 trucks?" Tom asked.

"Something like that is kind of plain vanilla. I think you're gonna be in the \$3,500 - \$4,500 monthly range. We can get it done in about 3 to 5 days," Jim said.

"Okay, let me finish up with the customer, and I will get back to you. Thanks," and Tom hung up. He returned to Mr. Anderson and explained the situation and the delay, although he left the pricing estimate given by Jim out of the conversation.

"Mr. Bennet, my boss would like to wrap this up this afternoon as it's the end of our quarter, and we would like to have this finalized," Anderson said with a furrowed brow. "What if we added \$10,000 monthly to the contract, and hopefully that covers all additional expenses?"

"Sure," Tom replied without having to think twice. "I'm sure I can make that work. Where do we sign?"

They finished up the paperwork which was pretty much already completed. They just made the adjustments that were discussed. Documents were signed and copied, and Tom shook hands with Anderson, departing with butterflies in his stomach. He couldn't wait to get out, wondering if something was going to go wrong or if the other shoe would drop.

When he got to his car, he called Jim to initiate the insurance and try to get the premiums delayed as much as possible until he received the first payment from the State. Jim had said he could pull this off with his insurance carriers, so everything was in motion. Things were beginning to look up.

Tom had one more call. "Lieutenant Sanders, good news. We have the truck fleet in place, and I will be able to begin the deliveries by the end of the week. I may need a little accommodation, however. Could we schedule the pick-ups and deliveries after normal hours? It would be better for us to work the night shift as there will be less traffic."

"Yeah, I think we can do that. Let me know your schedule, and I will alert security. I look forward to getting this rolling by the end of the week. Thank you," the lieutenant signed off.

"Yesssss," Tom was nodding his head up and down as he sat in his car. *Sometimes the Divine Universe opens its hand a little and lets the sunshine in*, he thought to himself, smiling.

Chapter 18

Delivery of an Important Message

Later that evening, Tom and Eve met up at Cheryl's home for another quiet evening, he hoped, to compare notes and explore further what his insights might mean.

After some light socializing, they lowered the lights, Cheryl lit some incense to create a calm mood, and they began to relax and enter a meditative state. Cheryl walked through the stages gently, talking in a mesmerizing manner to quiet the minds of all participants.

Tom began to quiet his mind. Some people joke it is like watching paint dry, but he stayed focused on the present and watched what was passing through that big screen, his mind, as an observer… viewing that there is more to what we see on the surface.

Then he just stopped. He turned his attention and focus to his left and looked at the entranceway of Cheryl's house, metaphorically because he had not moved his body, just his attention and focus. "That was pretty cool," he thought to himself, "the ability to move."

He decided to test it a little further and imagined himself floating up to the ceiling and looking down at the group in the living room, sort of like the exercise on the beach where he was watching himself and then entered himself and felt the sand under his legs and the wind on his body.

When he realized he was not in his body but looking at it, at least in his mind, the thought came to him, "Hey, this is amazing." At that, he whipped back into himself again, and the thought came to him, "If I'm reviewing my actions, then I am not in them. I am not in the present. I am looking at myself in the present, but I'm not in it." That thought was a revelation that there is a difference between being in the present and thinking of being in the present—an ever-subtle shift.

Tom started to experience that unpleasant feeling from the other day. It started quietly. First, it began like a sensation he was falling; then, the darkness became a void and with it a sense of aloneness so severe it was tuned to being abandoned by life itself.

Suddenly, the darkness shot up from below with a howling, horrific face so that Tom's hands shot up to protect his face and push this thing away with as much force as he could.

He heard a bang in the distance, and a flash of light was so bright it hurt, although his eyes were still shut. When the light subsided, the darkness was gone, and all seemed still... except for his shallow breathing. He heard voices in the distance, bringing him back to the reality of the room he was presently in.

Cheryl, Anita, and Eve moved about the room as he opened his eyes. He focused further and saw the room was in chaos, with a shattered lamp across the room and one of the side tables on its side.

Tom spoke for the first time, interrupting the ladies who were picking up the mess, "What's going on? What happened to the lamp and table?" he asked.

"Don't you know?" Anita asked, "You lifted your arms in a scream, and that lamp flew across the room. We've never seen anything like it."

Eve sat by Tom's side, looked him square in the face, and asked, "How did you do that? Did you see what you were doing?"

"All I saw was that horrific thing in a cloud of blackness jump at me so fast I shot my arms up to protect myself and push it back as hard as I could," he said. "It scared the hell out of me."

"Us too, Tommy boy. That was a heck of a show," Cheryl piped in.

"I'm sorry, Cheryl, I will replace the lamp. I don't know what came over me or how I could possibly have done this," he said.

"Don't worry about it. It wasn't like a family heirloom. What most concerns us all is how you did this," asked Cheryl.

"Hell, if I know, but I did feel a surge of something. I was so focused, like a laser beam, on that thing, and then, it was like all my Will and desire was on it to push it back. I'm exhausted." Tom took a moment to gather himself and then, "Maybe I should be getting along. I've caused enough disruption in your nice house. I'm sorry, Cheryl. Really."

He started to leave, and Eve walked him to the door. "Do you need some company to talk about it?" She asked.

"I think I need to walk this off and try to absorb what just happened," he said, "but thanks for your concern."

"Tom, before you go," Anita chimed in, "understand this is not a light thing. You have something, and these things don't just happen. There's usually a reason. Where much is given, much is expected. What needs to be understood is 'why' and what is expected. We can try to guide you to get this answer, but, in the end, you need to find it."

Tom nodded in gratitude but couldn't help but feel apprehensive about whatever spiritual journey he was on. He felt incredibly self-conscious too.

Eve walked out with him. She held his hand to comfort him. She looked up and said, "that must have been pretty scary." She waited a little, but no response came. "I can imagine that this might seem pretty frightening. You're not alone, although you might feel that way. We believe in you," she said, followed by a pause, and then, "I believe in you."

Perhaps the most powerful words in the Universe.

Tom decided he did need some fresh air, and the bayfront park which overlooked Biscayne Bay, was nearby enough to walk.

The evening was calm, and the temperature was pleasant. The walk had a soothing effect. When he arrived at the park entrance, he spotted a nice empty bench that faced the open bay. And nobody was near it… a bonus in his present state of mind. He walked straight to it, plopped down, and stared out at the open water.

What a roller coaster he was having. One moment things were looking up; the next, horror. On one side, it seemed the Divine Universe was sending a signal to follow a path to some success; then, he'd get slammed by something else.

What gives? And what was this eerie "thing" that kept creeping up on him? It was like a thousand cockroaches crawling on him, but from the inside, not on his skin. Then, in the periphery of his consciousness appeared a vacuum into a void so profound it blanketed him with a devastating sense of aloneness. If hell was a place, he could see how this could be it.

"You're not reading your messages," said the shabby-looking man who sat down next to him.

"Of all the places in the park…" Then it dawned on him. "Messenger, right?" Tom asked.

"The very same," he said.

"You look different," Tom said with a suspicious eye.

"Does it matter what shape I am in? When a message is delivered, do you care what the package looks like?" He added.

"I guess not," Tom replied.

"Well, that's some big bullshit, and you know it," the messenger retorted with a slight chuckle. "You very much weigh the importance and value of a message depending on who is delivering it. Ain't I right? C'mon, be honest with yourself. Who cares what I think? After all, I'm just some vagrant on the street. Right?" He was looking at Tom slightly turned and angled down a bit, then after a moment's pause, he asked, "Did you see the ads for lamps that were on sale that I sent you?"

Tom looked over to him with a question mark written on his face.

"Last Wednesday, at your breakfast? The table you sat in had a newspaper, which was folded to show the ad for the sale of lamps. Floor lamps, table lamps... don't you remember?"

"Maybe. Vaguely," said Tom. "So, what about it?"

"Don't you need to be replacing a lamp these days?" The messenger pressed on.

Tom's face took on a new look of astonishment.

"How about the cone that was holding a parking spot on Northwest 2nd avenue near mid-town? You moved it so you could get park closer to the event. Do you remember doing that at least?" Hammered the messenger.

"Yeah, I remember. Otherwise, I would have had to walk three more blocks, and someone left it there for no reason I could determine," Tom rebutted.

"That was clever thinking on your part. How's that left door on your car?" the messenger looked over again.

"Oh, man. That was you?" Tom moaned.

"That was me trying to help you. But you're thick, man. You are not paying attention to the signs presented under your very nose!" He was getting a little agitated, and Messenger then turned his body to face Tom. "You've broken through a layer of the cloud. You've upset some forces that get upset at these things. Forces that want to keep you, and the human race for that matter, in a dazed and confused state. This is good, but it is not without its challenges."

"What should I do?" Tom asked.

"I can't tell you what to do," Messenger replied. "That's why you have free Will, a conscience, and a soul. It is up to you. It is up to your Will and how you employ it. Some people throw their hands up and say it is fate. Others plow ahead and seek more."

"Are you my guardian angel?" Tom finally asked.

"No, I am a messenger," he replied and said nothing further.

They both said nothing for a while, then Tom asked, "Messenger, what shall become of me?"

"Whatever you want it to be," Messenger comforted. "Belief is the strongest force in this Universe."

Chapter 19

A Small, Unassuming Hero

"Phil, I'm going to need you to ride the inner side of the northwest 50 section," said the dispatcher.

Lieutenant Phillip Ames replied, "That's the little Haiti neighborhood. What's up with that?"

"We're short a few cruisers, and the captain asked for you," the dispatcher continued as he was handing out the daily schedules.

"Okay, it's not a problem. I just haven't done that route in a while," he said as he made notes on his roster.

Phillip Ames was a long-time patrolman for the Miami Police Department and had been offered a more senior position behind a desk many times. He preferred the motion of the streets and the interaction with his colleagues and the public.

He was promoted to lieutenant for his leadership abilities as well as his heroic performance on multiple occasions. Since he wouldn't accept an inside position, the department was delighted to have such a capable patrolman on the streets to cruise, supervise, and guide the rank and file in uniform.

He wrapped up his paperwork and headed for his designated car. An unmarked, specially prepared police cruiser with powerful engine, special tires, and state-of-the-art electronics.

The heat in Miami was scorching, so he had his air conditioning at full blast. With the uniform and the Kevlar bulletproof vest underneath, one could get pretty sweaty just sitting in the shade.

He left the station and slowly headed for his assigned sector. There was no rush. It was always good to take in the surroundings. See, and be seen.

He was moving through traffic northbound on Northwest 2nd avenue when there seemed to be some construction ahead; the already busy traffic began slowing down.

Lieutenant Ames decided to turn left on the next residential street and maneuver his way to his destination, routing through neighborhood streets. Residents in these parts were hard-working people, but with fewer means, often overlooked by both society and police. A show of the flag was always a good service, both for the would-be bad guys, as for the law-abiding residents.

The ride was going pleasantly, the air conditioning was doing its job and the chatter on the radio kept him entertained. Thankfully there were no emergencies in progress, although the chatter never ceased. Just before making a left down a quaint street...

SPLAT! BHAMMM!

He whipped his head to every window and mirror, and in his rearview, he saw that something had just hit his back window. It looked like someone had thrown some food, and it splattered across the entire back window.

He slammed on his brakes, put the cruiser in park, and jumped out, ready to give chase to the would-be delinquent.

Instead of an expected gang member with an attitude, Ames saw a young boy running toward him. He couldn't have been more than eight years old. As he approached, he noticed the boy was in tears.

"Pleezz, mister policeman, my mommy needs help. Pleeezzz, come now," he begged, grabbing Lieutenant Ames' hand and beginning to pull.

So much for unmarked cars. These cars were so plain with beefed-up tires and 50 antennas poking out of them, people seemed to spot them a mile away.

Ames didn't miss a beat and let himself be led by the young boy to the nearby house. He saw the front door was open to the small, slightly disheveled front yard.

As he approached the front door, his police instincts kicked in. *Is this a trap?* He considered. He didn't pull out his revolver, but he unlatched the safety and had his hand firmly on it.

The little boy already ran in, and when he noticed that Ames was not right behind, he returned to the door. But Ames was holding his position right outside the door. "Anybody inside?" Ames called out.

"Pleeezzz, she is very sick," the little boy pleaded.

Just then, Ames heard a groan and carefully but deftly crossed the threshold and stepped inside. He quickly scanned the room as he had done a thousand times in similar situations.

He then heard a loud moan and gurgling sound coming from the kitchen, and the little boy was at its entrance.

"This way, mister policeman," he insisted.

Realizing the situation was probably what it seemed, a person in distress, Lieutenant Ames rushed toward the kitchen. As he entered, he saw a woman, in her thirties on the floor. There was some blood, but he could not determine from where.

"Unit 546 request EMT service to 225 northwest 57th street. Subject appears unconscious and bleeding. Request child services as well," he barked into his portable radio.

"Unit 546, roger. Emergency medical has been requested and is on its way. Estimated arrival within four minutes from last reported position," the dispatcher responded.

Ames looked at the little boy, "What's your name?"

"I'm Billy and that's my mommy. Is she going to be okay?" The tears and worry on Billy's face were ripping at Ames' heartstrings.

"We're doing everything we can, Billy. You're a very brave boy coming to find me and saving your mom. The ambulance and doctors are on the way now."

Just then, they heard the ambulance pulling up outside the house. Ames stepped out of the kitchen holding little Billy's hand. "Let's give the doctors room to help mom. Okay, Billy?"

Billy was wide-eyed and nodded his head. The emergency team moved swiftly through the front door, and Ames pointed to the kitchen. Pros didn't need more than that.

The kitchen was a tight fit now with three people, the stretcher, and auxiliary medical devices, but within minutes they had an IV connected, an oxygen mask flowing, and a solid heartbeat. As they were wheeling the mom out, they looked at Ames and Billy and gave a thumbs up. One of the ambulance team pulled Ames to the side so that Billy was out of earshot, "It seems she fainted and hit her head. Why we can't say at this time, but we have a solid heartbeat, and there doesn't appear to be any hemorrhaging. It's a good thing we caught this on time. Whoever called it in may have saved her life." He then turned and helped his partner with the stretcher out of the house.

As they were leaving, a rather tall, good-looking thirty-something lady stepped aside to let them pass and then entered the house. Billy was visibly shaken up, and Lieutenant Ames was trying to comfort him as best he could.

"Hello, I'm Tina Cartwright with the child services department," she opened.

"Thanks for coming so promptly. As you just saw, that was our hero Billy's mom going through that door," Ames said, "As you can imagine, he is exhausted and worried. Can you take over, Tina?"

"Of course," Tina rushed forward, kneeling in front of Billy and bring him to her in a warm embrace.

Ames made his way to his cruiser now that he saw Billy was in good hands. He walked out the front door and noticed police backup that arrived while all the commotion was going on in the kitchen. The cruisers were keeping the neighbors and traffic at bay and doing some crowd control. These were his guys.

"Hey, Lieutenant," one of the officers nodded.

Ames nodded back. "A little excitement, but I think things are working out for this family."

"So, who fruited the back of your car?" Another patrolman piped in.

"Oh, that. I forgot. That's what got me to stop in the first place. What the hell is that anyway?" Ames asked, looking over at his car.

"It looks like mango to me. I like to take them differently but to each his own." All the cops started to laugh, but just as they looked at Ames, the laughter died down.

"Yeah, mango..." he said to himself, almost in a kind of haze. It dawned on him; that guy the other day that helped break up the crowd at mid-town, "... Mango alert, was that what he said?" He looked like he was seeing something in another dimension.

The backup team looked on at Ames curiously as he nodded and walked toward his car.

Chapter 20

To be Acknowledged and to be Loved

"So, you were going to tell me a little more about yourself," Tom started, looking directly at Eve.

"Uh, like what kind of stuff?" She responded as they were finding a seat at the little bakery-café.

"You know, all those interesting fun facts you normally leave out of your conversations," he edged on.

"Oh, you mean like when I buried my grandma in the basement? Or took my dad's car for a joy ride at one in the morning without permission?" She whispered, inching closer to his face, her eyebrows raised in a "you won't believe what I just saw" expression.

"Exaaaactly," Tom leaned in with a wicked smile, "the juicy stuff."

She leaned back in a prim and proper posture, "Oh, Mr. Bennet, I don't think I know you well enough for that," she said in her most prudish tone.

They both burst into laughter.

"It's not like they abandoned me or anything… it's just," they overheard a young woman at another table in the café speaking with her friend.

"It's just what, Pam?" Her friend Charlotte was moving in for more of her friend's family history.

"… It's just that they were always so busy with everything, and… there just didn't seem to be a lot of time for me," she finished staring into her own past with a saddened look on her face.

Eve and Tom were at a nearby table following the whole conversation but trying to be as innocuous as possible. They were both staring at their menus on the table with heads down and almost touching foreheads.

"Why are you two busybodies intruding on my customer's conversation?" Orlando whispered, sticking his head in between the two.

They both jumped back startled, which then caused them all to break out laughing!

When they had calmed down a bit, Tom looked at Orlando and asked, "What are you doing here?"

"I own the joint, bub!" Orlando replied with a *hey, is that a problem?* Look on his face.

Tom looked over at Eve, "Eve?! When were you going to say something?"

"I thought I told you the Buena Vista Bakery was Orlando's," she said.

"Well, if you did, I missed that part, but no matter, it's a cool place, Orlando," Tom said with a look of admiration and approval. One business owner to another.

It's no easy task to start and open a business. Even harder to make it succeed. Many people think just because you are a business you are just like a Wal-Mart. Not so, it's more complex than that!! There are employee issues, vendors, start-up funds, bank loans… if you can get them. There are lots of moving parts. So, when you can make it run smooth, you have, indeed, accomplished something. Usually at the cost of a lot of sleepless nights.

Orlando pulled up a chair. He had been in the back kitchen when he spotted the two up front, and, of course, he had to come out.

"What are you two doing here? Not that I'm not glad," he asked.

"Well, Tom came by to talk, and it was around lunch," Eve started.

Orlando looked at his watch, "Eve, it's three in the afternoon," he said with a *what the heck?!* expression, confirmed by the light crowd remaining in the small café.

"Alright, a very laaate lunch," she shot back with a laugh.

"Well, that's cool. I'm happy you took the break and came by. I have some, just made fruit tarts cooling down from the oven if you want to check them out," he said, then nodding his head over to the two girls at the other table, "but what was so fascinating across the way that had you two so enthralled?"

Eve looked at Tom, then back to Orlando, who was now sitting as a threesome. They crouched together with all three heads looking down at the table menus again, "One of the girls, let's call her, 'girl with issue'," she said, "was talking to her friend about being kind of ignored, or as she put it, abandoned, as a child. This caught my attention."

"Why?" Orlando asked, prodding a bit.

"I'm not sure. I think, perhaps 'cause we're all a little needy. I think I was too," she said. "We were just intrigued with the implications of that thought."

"I think what Eve is driving at is that we all need to be acknowledged. We need to feel we are loved… by someone. Anyone. It doesn't even have to be a parent. It seems that is innate in our human psyche. Even as adults. Why even the most important people we see, that we look to for guidance, that tell us how to live, surround themselves with people. They call them 'advisors'. Many are, but others are just 'yes' men in many cases and people to acknowledge them. What is your take on it?" Tom finally asked, looking over at Orlando.

"I suppose that is a fair assessment," Orlando said. "Which would bring us to what the love part of the equation is? *N'est pas*? Is it not so, as the Frenchies say?" He threw in.

"Ahh," Tom began after a pause, "That's always been the item people try to bottle up." He paused again, trying to compose his thought, "… if we consider that love brings a sense of well-being, a happiness, then…"

"—it is in the category of a feeling," Eve finished looking over at Tom.

"Yes, but to add to that," Tom interjected, "the love feeling also includes with it a sense of 'belonging'. That you're not alone. Initially, it is with your partner. The two are one…"

"—but then everyone," Eve added, "which is why people in love are the easiest to be with. They have a sense of inclusion and society," she finished.

They both looked at each other and high-fived one another.

Orlando was looking at these two like he was watching a tennis match; each finishing the other's sentence.

"Let me add a little something from experience," Orlando finally cut in, "when you start delving into yourself, that is, really moving in profound meditation, you may find what may, at first, appear as a void or another side. The other side is a completely encompassing and fulfilling sensation that fills you so completely it is not describable in words." He paused, then, "this is love in the most profound way because it is the Divine Love, your birthright… but that is not easy to achieve right away, and that path is treacherous and painful… as was appropriately stated, 'the examined life is not a picnic'." He paused again, reflecting. "… but I need to emphasize, this life experience is what it's all about. This reality. We need to experience this in the here and now. We need acknowledgment, inclusion, and love. If you're in for the experience, then you're in for the ride. All of it. The ups, the downs, the sideways. And during that ride, we need to be acknowledged. This motivates our sense of purpose with Love nourishing and uplifting us." He paused in contemplation.

The group was silent for a moment absorbing Orlando's valid thought.

He then continued, "I suppose that was this girl's angst across the other table. If you don't get this acknowledgment when you are the most vulnerable, as a child, you may miss out most of your life not thinking it even exists... since you never tasted it. A life of a lone raft in lonely waters. Yes, that would be very, very sad," Orlando said as he pondered his own statement. "Fortunately for me, I am one of six. Between all of them, I did get my share. Yeah, between bantering with them, but I love them all. And then, I have these crazy girls." He then paused looking at Eve with a grin. "But here I'm not sure if it's the fruit tarts, the croissants, or the Orlando?" he said mockingly.

Eve feigned a big gasp with an astonished expression of "not me" on her face.

Orlando started to get up, "Let me get those fruit tarts before we solve any more of the world's problems."

"He's quite special, Tom," Eve replied. "He seems very nonchalant, but I can't tell you how many emergencies he has gotten us all out of. But don't ask him. He'll deny it all. Sort of like an angel's helper with no name and no recognition, but to us, he's an unsung hero."

They chomped greedily on their fruit tarts when they arrived and headed back to Eve's shop soon after they finished.

Chapter 21

An Unseen Attack

"Okay, then Fred, if we can provide the transportation vehicles, you are saying we can do the logistic services for Tropical Produce?" Tom felt he had pushed a little more than he should have.

"No, I said you have a shot at doing it, and we would review your abilities, operations, and price," Fred Reyes shot back with a gentle grin of an accomplished negotiator and successful businessman in his own right. He liked Tom Bennet, but he was above any slick salesman tactic.

"Of course, Fred. Nothing is taken for granted,"... ah, how gracefully he backed off, maintaining his dignity and decorum. "The truck fleet would need to meet your specifications and actually solve a problem for you at a better cost."

"I don't have a problem, Tom... but I am open to other solutions," Fred returned with a "gotcha" grin.

"I will get back to you with something you are going to want. Let me rile my resources and put something together for you. And thanks for the opportunity, Fred. I mean it sincerely. I appreciate that you're taking a second look at this," Tom said.

"We haven't done business before, but I know you do good work for others. Let's be clear; this is a business deal. Whether I like you or not will not make the deal, but it is always pleasant to do business with someone you like." Fred let that hang in the air for a moment with the remainder unsaid… he liked Tom, but that would not be enough to put his money on him.

They both got up. The meeting and light lunch were over.

They looked each other in the eye, each acknowledging the other's worth as a sign of respect; it was not a challenge of any kind.

Tom headed for the exit and saw Fred taking a call on his cell phone and moving to the side.

As Tom made his way toward the small café's exit, he dovetailed behind a couple arguing about such stupidity, like who did the dishes last night and that kind of nonsense that Tom could not figure out if they were for real.

Tom looked over at who was speaking and he caught the girl's eyes. There was a rage there. She was having a meltdown, veins popping out of her temples and neck. This was thrombosis material, for sure. Good thing she was young.

He thought, *What could possibly be so important or detrimental to have someone go into a state like that?*

A certain clarity of thought came to him that we cover ourselves with layers upon layers of what we think is protection. Protection from what is another question. Certain psychiatrists and professionals call this our "ego." Tom thought of it as a cloud layer covering the soul.

We layer ourselves because we think we are not pretty (enough) or good-looking (enough) or rich enough (like that makes us more… anything). The layer will consist of purchasing outfits that boost our image or looks. What's inside is still the same, though. Sadly, it can get to a point we don't even remember what's inside.

Tom reflected on the thought of himself sitting in the auditorium, watching himself as a character in a play. How true this rang for this rage-filled girl. *Get out of character, hon,* he thought to himself. *Chill…* He had to laugh to himself.

He looked again, and the girl stared at him for a moment. In just those few seconds, it seemed that the temperature within her started to drop dramatically. She seemed to give an embarrassed sigh and slight tilt of her head like she was astonished at her performance. She turned back to her boyfriend or husband, took his arm in hers, and walked away. Every tempest runs its course.

He turned to walk in the opposite direction and what should have been the sidewalk café scene was an image that took up the whole of his frontal vision in a sort of vignette super-imposed on the reality around him. The vision was a giant image of the left corner of a mouth in a full downward snarl with teeth showing.

He was so caught off guard he just stared, and as he did so, the image zoomed back and widened so he could see the entire mouth. It was in full snarl mode. In rage mode.

The image widened even more and encompassed the entire face. It was hideous! But the eyes! The eyes transmitted everything. It was Hate like he had never seen. A Hate so consuming it deformed the features on the face... and there was a growling snarl sound coming from it... the air grew colder... He was mesmerized.

When he caught its eyes, the creature on the other side caught Tom's. This wasn't an image, like in a dream; this was in real-time. This was happening now.

The image pulled back further in a flash, and the creature had one arm extended toward him. At the end of the arm was a very sharp object.

Before he could process what he was seeing, the whole image lunged at him with the sharp object pointing to his heart.

Instantly, like a matador, Tom shifted his left side, pulling it back and narrowing his frontal exposure position. The creature's sharp object narrowly missed Tom's heart and hit his left arm.

"Yehowww!" Tom cried out as a piercing pain struck his left arm, snapping him into the day, a reality he was more used to.

At the same time this was happening, a waiter was walking toward him, negotiating his way through the outdoor tables. He was overburdened with clearing out a table on his tray. One hand balanced the tray; the other was grasping tightly to a bunch of utensils.

It all happened so fast. Because he could not see the floor or his feet due to all he was carrying, the waiter tripped over a handbag on the ground near another patron's chair. He lurched forward, trying to regain his balance, but it was too late. He was going to hit the floor. The waiter quickly moved his right hand, full of utensils, to try to get a two-hand grip on the tray. That's when the utensils went flying toward Tom, who was standing only a few feet away.

Tom seemed to be focused on something far away, but he moved deftly to one side, narrowing his exposed chest. There was not a whole lot of room to move, and a steak knife flew right into his left arm.

"Yeheoww!" Tom snapped out of his trance and looked at the back end of the knife hanging out of his arm.

It was a freak accident, and almost impossible for a knife to fly from the waiter's grip and have enough impact to penetrate skin and flesh. It was almost as if it had a helping hand. Something pushing on it. The waiter looked up and was aghast!

"Oh my god!" The woman at the table next to him cried out. "Someone get this man some help."

Although she stood up to help Tom, she didn't know whether to grab the knife or Tom. She had her napkin in hand to help with the now dripping blood.

"It doesn't look too bad," said Tom as he gently began to extract the knife from his arm. He made a pained face but managed to withhold any groans as he didn't want to look like a weakling. It hurt like hell, though, and a tear welled up as he gave the last pull. That's when it really started to bleed.

The waiter had already stood up and the manager had run out after the commotion trying to calm the patrons around the tables. The general public had remained relatively calm, and for the most part, remained in their seats.

Tom sat with the lady that had stood by with the napkin. "Thank you so much. I usually try to avoid a knife fight," he added with a charming smile and a question mark on his face.

"Natasha," she said. "And this is my friend Carrie. We were just commenting on what a pleasant and tranquil place this is." She began laughing and nodding to Carrie.

The manager rushed to Tom with apologies, trying to see what he could do to smooth things over. He called for assistance from his workers, towels for Tom's injury, and ordered some beverages for Tom, the tables with the girls, and all in the outside patio.

"Please, it was an accident, and I'm okay. If you have some bandages, I think this will clean up fine. I could use another shirt, though," he looked up at the manager with a coy smile.

"A shirt, dinner, champagne, sir—whatever you like," the manager blurted out. He could not be more accommodating, only wishing this day would come to an end.

Tom smiled and looked at the manager, then at Natasha and Carrie, and said, "Okay. I'll take you up on the dinner, and I would like to invite my new friends."

They giggled and smiled. "Sure, we're in," they both said in unison.

"But it needs to be another time, folks," Tom said as he began to stand up. "I was actually running late for an appointment. Shall we say Friday? That will give me time to clean up and recover a bit," he added, maintaining his charming smile.

The girls looked at each other, then back at Tom, and nodded in agreement with a "look what we found" coquettish grin on their faces.

Great, he thought, *a date and on the house! Just what one needs to get when on a budget.*

Everyone agreed on the plan, and Tom rose to leave. He said his goodbyes and proceeded to walk down the sidewalk to his car.

As he approached the corner, a man with a fedora was standing close by. The hat made him appear well dressed; the rest of his attire screamed yesterday's news.

He was an odd-looking fellow, almost like a caricature. It was like he belonged in another century. His face had sharp-cut features and was slightly unshaven but not like a homeless type.

"Next time, it may not miss," he said.

"Beware," he said. "You've aroused the wrong forces…" He was looking straight into Tom's eyes.

Tom was taken aback. "Who are you? What do you mean? What forces?"

"Beware!" And just like he appeared, he turned sideways and melted into the crowd. Tom looked again, but he was nowhere to be seen.

Tom looked back toward the tables, then around him, to see if the caricature man had, by chance, been talking to someone behind him, but he was alone. When he turned back to try another look for the fedora, he was gone.

Where are you? He thought to himself. *Where did you come from?*

Chapter 22

The Other Shoe Drops Yet Again

When Tom arrived back at his bungalow behind Armando's, he found a man waiting for him by his door with a sachet-style bag on his left shoulder.

As Tom approached, he asked, "Can I help you with something?" "Are you Thomas Bennet?" He asked.

Oh boy, here we go, thought Tom. "Yes, I am."

"I have some papers for you," he said, handing them to Tom. Then he scribbled some notes on his ledger to confirm the server process date and time.

Just as the man left, Tom started to look over the first page. It was a summons. He was the target of a criminal investigation related to the Tampa Bank financial "irregularities." "Oh, fuck me!" He sighed. *When will this shit storm end?* He thought.

He grabbed the mail from the box and went into his little pad. *At least this offers a respite from life's torments*, he thought.

A letter caught his eye from the stack. It was from an attorney and looked official. He opened it first. His wife had filed a lawsuit for divorce.

As the Billy Joel song states, "Captain Jack will take you that special island," and that's where Tom went that night.

Chapter 23

A Friendly Connection

After dropping the kids off at school with the lunches he had made earlier, Tom headed for the vehicle depot to meet with Jim, his insurance agent, and get that paperwork in order.

He initiated the introductions to the person in charge of the depot but left Jim to register all the vehicle information, take his photos, and document what was needed. Tom would only be in the way as this was Jim's insurance company business.

He then headed to Eve's shop and picked up some coffee and pastries along the way.

"Hey, how have you been?" Eve greeted him as he entered her shop a little later.

"A little busy but moving forward. Two steps forward, one step back. I brought us a little something if you haven't had breakfast yet and have a few minutes."

She snatched the bag with a grin and looked in. "Ohhhh, pastelitos and croquetas! You must want something really bad," she said with a laugh.

"Actually, just a little pleasant company," Tom said.

"Ahhh, how sweet," her reply landed somewhere between a little sarcastic and, "I'm not buying it."

She bit into the croqueta, closed her eyes, and sighed. "These are sooo good. Where did you get them?" She asked while wiping her hands from the croqueta crumbs and reached for the café con leche.

"There's a little bodega coming down 8th street that's run by the same mom and pop for years. Price is right, and they make them themselves," he said.

As they were munching on their breakfast, she began asking Tom how he was doing with all his comings and goings. Tom related everything happening to him, taking a little extra time on the almost supernatural events that were occurring with more frequency. On one side, some mildly good things, on another, some potentially explosively bad things.

He further quipped how he didn't understand if this was some kind of karma as he thought he had been a relatively okay person. He was no saint, but he didn't feel the karma level, if that was indeed the payback he was getting, was warranted by possible previous behavior on his part. *Well, that's what we all think of ourselves*, he thought.

"Maybe you should go see my friend Dora," Eve finally volunteered.

"What... is she some bruja?" Tom asked.

"No, she's not a witch, for god's sake! Nor is she into the Santeria. You know, that Cuban mysticism?" She said. "But, I don't know, she has a gift. She sees things. She has helped me many times, and I have sent her a few friends who love her. She might help."

Can't lose for tryin', he thought and accepted Dora's phone number.

Tom called Dora later that day, and it just so happened she was free that afternoon. She gave Tom her home address to come by later. And he did.

Chapter 24

Dora the Occult Explorer

Dora greeted Tom when she answered her door.

It was an ordinary home in the central part of old Miami. No red curtains, nor crystal ball or incense. Just a regular-looking home occupied by a regular-looking, grandmotherly type woman with a calm and soothing demeanor.

She asked if he wanted anything to drink or eat. "A coffee, water?"

Tom declined respectfully.

She then guided him to a back room with two chairs and a series of religious artifacts sprinkled about. They sat down facing each other, and she stared at him for a few minutes.

Dora spoke first. "You are either the driver or the rider. If you decide to drive, then you must lead and fight back the dark forces."

Eve was right; this lady hit direct targets.

"But how? I feel like a shadow boxer. I don't know where the next punch is coming from. Where do I go to meet the enemy?" he asked.

"Your five senses are your portal to this material world. These are how you know you are alive in this world, but they don't make you alive. Calm down your senses and what remains is You, the essence of your being, and you will be in that space. A space you can move toward the light or the darkness. To fight darkness, you must confront it. Do not be afraid of it, as you are more powerful than it. Use the material plain like it does. All the resources of the Universe are yours if you know how to ask for them."

"Quieting your mind to the point of vacant is not easy," Tom responded.

"No, it is not. It is the hardest thing you will ever accomplish, but to seek what you are looking for requires extraordinary efforts. Milk is for children, meat for adults," Dora continued. "You might not be able to influence natural forces on the material plane, but you are clever, and you can use the resources about you in your favor to counter and evade what the dark forces block in your way. Do not be afraid, and you will triumph. But do not be deceived, for always there will be greater and lesser than yourself. Know yourself. If you are a sparrow, don't try to do the things an eagle does. Yet even the carrion birds get to eat the whole zebra after the lion's kill." She went silent for a moment. "This is everyone's right and within everyone's abilities. We just have seen many wishing to be riders,"

It was as if she were speaking in parables. It took him a little to unscramble her meaning and absorb the impact of the information she was spewing. But these were the gems one finds in the dirt, no doubt.

A little later, while walking out of Dora's place, his mind someplace else, Tom's phone rang. As he answered, he was greeted immediately with, "Mr. Bennet, good afternoon; this is Mike Alvarez with Logistics Trucking. Do you remember me?"

"Sure Mike, you sold me some equipment some time back. What's up with you these days?" Tom asked politely.

"I know we haven't spoken in some time. I'm calling to see how your truck fleet is these days," Mike replied.

"Well, it's non-existent, Mike. I had some setbacks, and I'm presently re-grouping. Why do you ask?"

"We got a cancellation on a big order of trucks, and we're sort of over-stocked. The customer lost the large deposit, so we are able to offer an excellent deal. Since you are an old customer, I called you first," Mike offered.

"Well, curiously, I just landed a deal that requires some trucks, but the fleet was included in the deal, so I can't use your offer at the moment. I will keep it in mind if something comes up, however," Tom said.

"Okay, sir. Thanks for the clarification. Please don't hesitate to call. My manager is willing to wheel and deal on this one," Mike finished.

"Understood. Thanks for keeping me in mind, Mike," Tom said as he finished the call.

Always when you don't need it, he thought.

Chapter 25

An Old Friend and Ally

"Patty," Tom spoke as soon as the phone was answered.

"Hey, where has my favorite client been?" She retorted. "It seems you only call when you're about to go to jail or have the government crawling down your back." Tom could tell from the sound of her voice she was having fun with this.

Patty Amores was Tom's long-time attorney and confidant. She had pulled him out of more near misses (actually, near crashes) than he could count. She was a bulldog in court and knew her law better than most litigation attorneys, which was why she was so good in court.

You didn't want to be opposing counsel against Patricia Amores, Esq. Tom was glad to have her as his corporate, personal attorney and a good friend to boot.

"Well, don't take it personally, but as you know, I've had the rug pulled from under me," Tom added. "I've been in the loop. I didn't call because I figured you had a lot on your plate, and you have my number. You know I am here for you. How are the kids?" She always asked about the kids.

"The kids are great, thanks. You know, the wife called it quits, but I manage to pick them up at school every day, and I have them over several times a week. We're growing up together, so it's good."

"So, what's up? How are you fairing these days?" She asked.

"It's up and down. On one side, I have managed to finagle a small contract with the State that Armando helped me land, but there are rumblings on another end. I think the feds are trying to do something. Remember the First Financial of Tampa deal?"

"Of course, I worked out the kinks in the paperwork. It was a terrible contract. How can I forget?" Patty replied. "What's wrong with it?"

"Nothing is wrong with it, but now they have come back accusing misconduct, stating monies are missing. They canceled the line, which caused me to withdraw my already approved contract with the government and, I believe, referred the case to the Department of Treasury, which means the Department of Justice," Tom finished with frustration clearly in his tone.

"Well, did you steal anything? Where's my invite on the yacht?" She came back without missing a beat.

"Patty!" Tom sighed.

"All right, all right. Keep your panties on, Jeezz. What does your accountant say?" She asked.

"I can't find him. I am not sure where he is, and he is not answering his phone," Tom said.

"Okay, let me have access to your books, and I'll take a look. It just so happens I am wrapping up a big case, and I have a little time. Let me make some inquiries with some friends at the DOJ and see what's surfacing," she said. Of course, it helped that Patty had worked with the financial crimes unit for the feds and the state after graduating from law school. She knew all the maneuvers, where to look, and how to find things... if they were missing.

"DOJ?"

"Department of Justice, Tom. C'mon, get with the program and acronyms. And you say you work with government?" She shot back, teasing him a little. She loved the parry.

"Oh, of course, I'm just a little rattled is all. Let's talk after you've had a chance to get a handle on this. And thanks, Patty," he said as he finished the conversation. He felt a slight sense of relief after talking with her. Not that she had solved anything yet, but with Patty on the warpath in his favor, he felt less alone. Furthermore, the courts and the government had a lot of respect for her, so if she was making the inquiries, it brought a sense of a respectable business enterprise to the table and not some flim-flam operation.

Chapter 26

Patricia Amores, Attorney at Law

Patricia Amores was the youngest of four with three older brothers. At a very young age, she learned to eat or be eaten as her older siblings treated her as "one of the guys" and played rough with her accordingly. That was at home. To the outside world, no one was allowed to mess with their younger sister, or they'd have to deal with the consequences.

She played tag football with them… and won often since she was smaller, faster, and more agile. So much so that when teams were choosing players, she usually got picked first as their secret weapon. She loved the comradery.

Patricia was good in school but better at sports and outside activities. When she graduated college, she was drawn to the commodities exchange at the behest of her brothers, who were already very much involved in various aspects of the markets.

The fast movements, exchanges, and commotions were so similar to her life growing up; she took to it like a duck to water. She liked best the floor of the exchange where all the action happened.

Initially, she worked with the assistant team for the traders on the floor, but one day one of the traders became sick, and her boss asked her to process a few bids.

One would think her short size and being a woman would have buried her in the crowd, but the opposite turned out to be true. Her aggressive and fierce shouting got attention, and the client's order was sold at an unexpectedly better price than expected. Her boss was pleased.

She was allowed more and more on the floor to the point she became a regular on the trading team.

It was around this time her brother Ned became embroiled in an incident at the exchange. A sting operation by the Securities and Exchange Commission had been brewing for some time, targeting traders who were skimming and colluding with the trades. Ned swore to her he was not directly involved, but since he worked with several of the implicated traders, he got sucked into the mess.

During her ordeal, Patty was by his side and dealt with the legal counsel representing Ned. The process, the court, the protocols, and the use of the law to maneuver through the regulations piqued her interest. The law bug bit her.

She decided the commodities trader game might be fun, but like a football player's career, it was short-lived and hard for wear and tear. She decided to pursue law and began classes at night after work.

This time, she was not an average student with her full attention and interest in the subject matter. She aced all the classes, and when it came time to apply for law school, she had the recommendations of several of her professors. She was accepted at the University of Miami law school, which was perfect as it was near her home turf. She received a partial scholarship which eased the financial burden of what is a very costly institution. Yeah, student loans were plentiful, but little or no debt when you finished was much more attractive.

After graduation, she began with a litigation firm. Many of her peers pursued real estate law and corporate, but Patty's interest was always confrontation. That's where she excelled—on the sports field, in school, and on the trading floor. So, she was a natural in court defending her clients.

With their tedious research assignments, the ball-buster professors at law school paid off outside the classroom. Patty was always the most prepared on the courtroom floor with background information on the opposing party, conflicting information that placed a shadow of doubt on the case itself, and, of course, detailed knowledge of the law and precedents of relevant cases that, many times, knocked out the opponent's case altogether.

She was revered by her peers as well as the judges. She had already been considered for a judgeship, but for the moment, she had pushed this away.

Chapter 27

The Invisible Hand Pokes at Cheryl

It happened rather fast and when she least expected.

Sometime after Cheryl's "incident" in her room that night when something rubbed her foot, she began to be more alert of this possibility. The possibility that there was something else out there.

She was raised a Roman Catholic, so her religious studies, of course, believed in the afterlife or the beyond. She did as well. But it's one thing to wholeheartedly believe your soul will survive and move on after you die, and another thing to believe that in the here and now, there is another dimension that crosses into this reality. Ghosts, the macabre, and the unearthly things that can appear and do physical things to you.

After she finished high school and went on to a junior college, Cheryl was exposed to a wider variety of people. It was here that she first met some friends, that when she told the tale of the playing card stroking her foot experience on one of those intimate Friday night gatherings, the story was neither laughed at nor scoffed. On the contrary, her friends were also intrigued and wanted to pursue it further with Cheryl.

It started benignly enough on weekend nights. They all did some research during the previous week and then met up on the weekend to compare notes.

After a while, they decided to test things out. Again, it started out innocently enough with a "prayer" calling forth a spirit or a guide. Each had a ritual protocol. Some required the use of some herb or the burning of some incense in a censer.

One Saturday night, the three friends were huddled in Cheryl's room. It was about eleven in the evening, and it was still warm fall weather. It seemed to Cheryl the temperature in the room dropped a bit to the point she got a chill. Goosebumps. It was like someone lightly passed the tip of their finger up her spine.

She stirred and did a quick intake of breath. She opened her eyes quickly. Emily and Heather were looking at her.

"Did you feel that?" Cheryl asked.

"No, I just heard you gasp," Heather said.

"I thought I felt the room temperature drop, but I thought it was my imagination. Did you feel it too?" Emily asked Cheryl.

"Yeah, and something more. Like something touched me. Let's close this out for the night. I'm a little freaked out." Cheryl let out a nervous laugh trying to make light of it. But she was a little shaken up.

They were so disturbed by what they experienced the three left this alone for a while until one day at school, Terry Laugnor, one of the few wanna-be popular girls with her little click of groupies, humiliated Emily at the cafeteria.

In the scheme of things, and looking back, it was not an important incident, but it left Emily in tears, and other students shied away from her. No one had come to her defense.

Cheryl learned about it later, and to cheer her up, she said, "Let's do a little voodoo on her!" They both giggled and agreed they would.

That Friday night, the three met at Cheryl's and evoked the last ritual which had created the stir. They focused their energies to create some damage to Terry Laugnor's property; to humiliate her in some way.

The next day at the home football game, all three were seated in the bleachers watching the game. They noticed Terry in a lower section closer to the field, surrounded by her groupies and some of the more popular guys.

She was cheering at a passing run their team had done when her dress ripped from below her armpit to her thigh, unraveling it like a flap opening up. All the guys started laughing. People nearby started pointing and snickering.

If Terry would have been a tomboy type, this could have gone in her favor, but since she had an air about her, she was above hoi polloi and this was not a welcome event.

The three watched her turn three shades of red as she tried in vain to wrap the tattering of her dress around herself for cover. It didn't work. Cheryl, Emily, and Heather high-fived each other and were laughing hysterically as Terry ran out of the stadium.

"Hello," Cheryl answered the phone and heard sobbing on the other end, "Did you hear what happened?" It was Heather.

"No, what?"

"Emily is in the hospital. She was in a car wreck," she said, her voice cracking, and burst into tears again.

"Oh my god! How? What happened?" Cheryl demanded.

"I don't know. Her mom just called me. She's in bad shape."

"I'll pick you up in fifteen minutes. Get the details of where she is so we can go see her."

Emily pulled through, although not unscathed. Let's say that skirts would not be part of her most favorable outfits with the thick scarring on her legs. She also came away with a slight limp, but the doctors said that, with exercise, she could work through it.

They ended any further Friday sessions, but Cheryl never forgot. Nor did she forgive. It was a prank, not a nonconsensual lobotomy. If one thing was related to the other, the hand came down way too hard. She carried on with the assumption the two events were related.

She realized then there really were other forces out there… and they could be very mean and spiteful.

Chapter 28

The Messenger Returns

"Ahh, the messenger," Tom said, a little sarcastic giving the visitor a mock sense of importance. "I guess you're here to tell me how beautiful I am and that I'm wonderful and one of God's beloved creatures."

The messenger looked over with an expression that said, "This asshole didn't just ask me the stupidest question. Did he?" Instead, he said, "You're a little full of yourself, don't you think? That kind of fairytale thinking is for the movies or one of those uplifting songs about how great you are. So far, you are just a shit."

Tom looked a little shocked by this candid revelation. This guy didn't sugarcoat things, that's for sure.

"You are like a seed," continued the messenger, "full of promise and potential as any seed offers. But if it remains in the seed bin, then it will continue to only be a seed."

Tom looked over.

"Get yourself into some decent soil, which doesn't have to be the best. Get some regular water, which doesn't need to be from a special spring. With some effort, you will grow and flower to your full potential, and the promise that is yours as that seed. No one can take that from you. But you need to reach for it. Just reach, and the Divine

Universe will help you. Not a handout, though. Just reach, man. Just reach."

The inspiring words had Tom gently shaking his head.

"But what have you done to earn that? What have you created today with all the power, potential, and promise within you?" He looked and waited, watching Tom's astonished and embarrassed expression. "That's what I thought. That's why you're here moping."

Tom was taken aback by the messenger's aggressive rhetoric. It was like he was being scolded. One either thinks of themselves as the center of the universe or as unworthy. Ironically, this person who feels the latter is usually the worthiest of the two.

"Remember the story I told you about the guy who wants to be a doctor? That he is presented with a sighting for essentially no payment for his schooling at the start of his journey to be a doctor?"

"Yes, so what does that have to do with me?" Tom asked. "Look, friend, I'm at the end of my rope here. Shit is hitting the fan daily, and you're telling me stories about seeds and soil. If the great Divine Universe is so abundant and beneficial, then it could throw me a little help, a bone, don't you think?"

Messenger continued as if he had not heard anything Tom just said. "You're the guy at the end of the story. You need to be whacked over your head with a two-by-four and have your car break down in the rain to get your attention. Some people get it at the first sign, but our bright lad here, noo siree—not our boy wonder." The messenger went quiet and looked out.

Tom was about to add something in his defense.

After a few moments, he continued. "You have stepped off the path of sheep. You have asked, perhaps subconsciously, for something more, For Truth. You have to want this like a drowning man wants a gasp of air. Mother's milk is for babies, but you are looking for meat. It's hard. The hardest thing you will do in this life, but the reward is the greatest achievement offered to mankind."

Tom had his full focus on him.

"If you continue to pursue it, understand you are going against dark forces that want to keep you, and the human race, for that matter, stepped on. In a fog, blinded and lost, where darkness can offer their version of satisfaction. But it is like a potato chip, delicious to eat, but as soon as you swallow, you are looking for more. Yes, you are never satisfied, and here is where darkness feeds. Where one continues to go deeper and further away from their true spirit."

Tom nodded. He was beginning to get the message.

"You have opened a portal to your heart, but what is most astonishing is that your energy shows others the same path to their hearts. Darkness wants to take you out before you disrupt too much of their show. You need to fight or back down. Decide what you are going to do." The messenger was now looking straight into Tom's eyes."

Tom looked like a deer caught in headlights. The gauntlet had been thrown.

"The Light will be with you, and, more importantly, the Light within you is stronger than the Darkness. You must believe this is true. You must own this. Otherwise, you will fall. You will fail." He sat back again.

After a long silence, Tom stared out and asked, "What can happen to me? How far can they take this?"

"You can die. Loved ones near you can suffer or even die as well. Your life on this plane, as you know it with money, home, and all the other material comforts, can be made to suffer. The suffering of the material is only proportional to the value you put on it, of course. Concerning life and limb, know that your spirit is eternal, but it resides on this material plane, and if you crash against the rocks you will break."

After a long pause to consider the message, Tom finally spoke with a slightly sarcastic tone, "Ahh, it sounds so tempting what you offer. Damn it, if you're not the most depressing thing I've come across lately."

"A diamond is a rough and not-so-attractive stone," the messenger replied in a gentle and comforting tone. "But with grinding, some chiseling, and polishing it is the most coveted stone on the planet. It has cosmetic beauty and has other essential uses for humanity. Do you think the diamond getting ground doesn't hurt it if it could talk? Yet, look at the results."

He considered the comparison.

"It's not my offer, nor mine to offer." Messenger added after a slight pause, "You are presented with a choice. This is where your free Will comes in. You take it with consequences or choose not to take it with consequences."

Chapter 29

Light Replaces Darkness...For a Little While

On his way home from his seaside adventure with Messenger, Tom's cell phone rang. He grabbed it without looking at the caller ID because he didn't want to take his eyes off the road.

"Hey Tom, it's Eve."

He instantly felt a wave of happiness just hearing her voice. "Hey, you. What has you calling at this hour?" He asked.

"I was wondering if you caught up with Dora finally?" She asked.

"Yeah, I did. She's very nice. Not what I expected... on a lot of levels, actually."

"What do you mean?" She asked.

"Well, she appears someone's sweet little old grandma, but she is some powerhouse. And you were right; she brought perspective and a little insight. I owe you," Tom chuckled a little.

"Okay, then you can start paying up now," she laughed. "We're having a little sit-in with the girls. Cheryl thinks we need a fourth. Can you come over now?"

"Now? It's ten thirty on a Tuesday," he said a little too hastily.

"C'mon, Tom, it's not past your bedtime is it? We are trying to do a session that requires four." She sounded a bit disappointed, and Tom was grateful to her and the girls, and the last thing he wanted was to be on their "disappointment" list.

"Sure, of course. Let me take the next exit, and I will head on over. I think about twenty minutes. Are you there already, or should I pick you up somewhere?" he asked.

"No, I'm already here, thanks," she said. "Hurry but don't crash. See you shortly, and thanks again."

Tom made it in twenty-three minutes, but it took him another five to park and walk up to the house. When he knocked, the door was opened almost immediately, and Eve looking directly at him.

"Good evening, kind sir. So good of you to come on such short notice." She greeted him with a proper curtsy, a slightly exaggerated English accent, and a wide smile. Then, she laughed.

Tom grinned and nodded. "So, what's going on with you girls?"

"We were working on an exercise and thought we needed more energy in the circle. We thought of your lamp-throwing abilities," she said with her head tilted a little and a devious grin.

"Very funny... but not. And I already said I was sorry and would replace the lamp." He entered the foyer and spotted Cheryl.

Cheryl had a "don't look at me" face, shrugged her shoulders, and said, "... and we're all appreciative. Don't listen to her, Tom. She just wanted to get you over here," she chuckled.

"Cheryl!" Eve, now blushing, looked at her with "what are you saying?!" Eyes.

"All kidding aside," Cheryl said. "I think you might get something out of this; we all might. Communal meditation is a powerful process and may open passages that are otherwise blocked. The force of four is stronger than one. Let's try it?" Cheryl raised an eyebrow as if asking for permission.

"Yes," Tom responded, "I think I could use a little 'communal' for a change."

And so, they all sat in a circle and held hands.

Cheryl began by invoking a prayer requesting guidance and success from the Divine Providence and the Angels about us. Then, she started a low-level monotonous chant. It was a repetitive tone. Soon the other members joined in, finally followed by Tom.

They continued the chant, which brought a focus to the present moment. By chanting, one's mind does not drift as easily as you are focusing on the chant. And in the focus on a single point, you stay in the present.

As if on cue, they all stopped, and silence dominated the room.

At that very same moment, Tom, who had been focusing on his breathing while chanting, began to fade away his senses by not thinking about them at all. He drifted back and forth. One moment he thought, "Oh, I am in the NOW," except by thinking that he was no longer in it but observing it. So, he moved back into the moment. He knew what to look for now that he'd touched it.

He was floating and began to develop a sense of aloneness and that there was something in the periphery he did not want. Reaching from within, he began to feel an energy. He slipped back realizing he was observing himself rather than being himself. He chanted to himself, "I am present," and the space around him began to lighten a little.

He could not place where the light was coming from, but it was overtaking the foreboding feeling he had felt on the periphery of his senses earlier.

Then he realized the light was coming from the center, which is why he could not see its source.

However, he couldn't seem to be able to make the light stronger. It occurred to him that he was not alone but part of something beyond his comprehension. A sense of belonging suddenly overtook him, and he was flooded with an overwhelming sense of love. An unconditional love that asked for nothing from him and poured out to him.

Gathering a feeling from within rather than a thought, he knew he had friends about, and he called upon them for their energy.

He then felt additional energy join him, and the light became exceedingly bright around him. Any darkness in the fray disappeared.

"Om, om, om," he began on the fringes of his omni-sense of vision.

"Tom, Tom, come back to us."

He now heard the voice clearer. It was Eve gently rubbing his arm. He opened his eyes and slowly scanned the room. Eve was looking at him, as was Cheryl. Anita still had her eyes closed.

"What did you feel?" Cheryl asked. "You had a very peaceful look on your face. You were almost glowing. We all felt something uplifting."

He opened his mouth to speak. "I... I'm...." But he could not say anything.

"Don't," she said. "That experience is personal and for you only. I didn't mean to pry."

Tom nodded as he looked at her. "Thank you," was all he managed to say. Was it "thank you" for her last comment? For calling him tonight to participate? For sharing their energy to allow him to propel himself if that is indeed what happened? He couldn't say, but he was grateful for their presence nonetheless.

Tom stood and nodded again to the three ladies in the room. Everyone clearly understood the gesture as "thank you" and "goodnight."

His legs were like spaghetti as he half walked, half stumbled out of the house.

Chapter 30

Tom May Have Saved a Life

"Hello, Mr. Bennet?"

"Yes, this is he," Tom answered. *Here we go, first thing in the morning!* he thought with exasperation.

"I'm sorry to bother you. My name is Angela Corning. You stopped by my table at the La Tacita café on Bird Road," she pressed on, "… and asked me not to think you were crazy but to have my chest or abdomen area checked. Well, yes, I thought you were a little crazy and a little out of line since I felt fine, but later I told my boyfriend what happened, and he insisted I go to my doctor."

Tom remembered exactly who this was.

Angela continued. "Well, the MRI shows a tumor, and I am having emergency surgery this afternoon. It seems it is at such an early stage that they will get whatever it is. My doctor still doesn't understand how I felt anything since it is so small. Anyway, you asked me to call. I would've anyway. I don't know what gift you have, but I'm grateful for it and wanted to thank you for coming up to me." Her voice was a little shaky at the end, likely because of the gravity of what was going on in her life.

Tom was a little mystified and didn't respond right away. He was expecting another bad news call again this morning, and here came this miracle story instead.

"Hello, are you still there?" Angela finally asked after several moments of silence.

"Oh, yeah," he cleared his throat, "I'm… I'm sorry… I was just startled and overwhelmed by what you said. I am floored, actually. I'm sorry for your tumor, but thrilled they caught it so soon. The funny thing is I have never walked up to a stranger like that before. I don't know what came over me to do that with you, but I'm so glad I did."

"That's funny," Angela replied. "My uncle always said thoughts come into people's heads all the time, but so often, we don't act on them. We overthink it. Then, when we decide to do something about it, the moment passed… and we don't say anything. You know what I mean? I'm glad you didn't hold back. Who knows, maybe you saved my life." She giggled a little to lighten what she said a little, but she was as serious as a heart attack.

"Angela, you made my day for sure. Maybe my month or even whole year," Tom said, laughing at the end. "Please let me know how things turn out… and thank you very much for the call. You have no idea how much you have made my day."

Tom remembered that morning well. He was sitting at his table at the café, having his café con leche and tostada, the Cuban bread slathered with butter and toasted on an iron press grill. Something compelled him to look over, and he saw Angela. She was pretty, so looking over would not have been unusual, but this was different. It was like a magnetic pull. At the time, he did not think about it that way; it just was a natural movement to look around the restaurant.

Something specific caught his eye, though. He couldn't initially place it, but the scene with Angela looked different than it should. Sort of like when you see glare on an object, but this was the reverse. It was a darkness that distorted Angela's image. And just a portion of her; her belly area. Like a photo with bad lighting. It just didn't look right.

It was just like Angela's uncle said; he was not going to say anything, but then something within wouldn't let go and he went over to her.

Tom thought about that moment and remembered he was blank. The chatter in his head was on a low for some reason. Was he listening to his soul just then?

His grandmother had always told him, "If you're talking, you're not listening," which means listening to your own spirit source, which talks to you all the time.

Yeah, he was starting to get that.

Chapter 31

Ellie May... Or May Not

Elinore May Ramirez, known to Tom as Ellie May, had arrived at Tom's office via an ad placement. She was interviewed by the sales manager and began working in that department as a sales associate for the Bennet Company.

Both in the office and at client locations, Ellie proved to be one of the more astute salespeople the company had. She was charming and personable, as well as sharp-witted. She was smart and picked up on the Bennet product line and how it could be best applied to the customer. The fact she was quite physically attractive did not hurt how she performed at her job.

She was a hit on all accounts and month after month was the company's top salesperson. She was making a lot of money.

Tom and Ellie May met at a company picnic held at the local beach. She caught Tom's eye immediately when he saw her interacting with her colleagues from the company. She was the center of attention, pulling on everyone else like a magnet. She had their undivided attention in whatever story she was telling, and their faces showed it.

Tom approached the table wondering what all the fascination was about and caught the tail end of her story. As she was finishing up the crowd was laughing or audibly expressing their disbelief, "No way; you gotta be kidding!"

As for Ellie May, she was just smirking and laughing in tandem, saying, "I told you it was going to be hard to believe…" She was a natural storyteller, and people loved it.

A dear mentor once told Tom, "… don't dip your pen in the company inkwell." But he decided not to follow that advice.

He initially invited Ellie to lunch with some of the salespeople. Diluting the company made it less obvious he wanted to see more of her. Then, he attended some happy hour get-togethers with his sales team that he had rarely gone to. But with Ellie there, the allure changed.

The two of them started formally dating after a while. Tom even invited Ellie to several overnight business trips and made a mini-vacation out of it. Their romantic involvement was undeniable.

After almost two years, Tom finally proposed, and Ellie May Ramirez accepted.

They continued a life as "singles" traveling freely and without care until, one day, Ellie found out she was pregnant. They were both thrilled, and a new adventure began.

Isa was born at 4 a.m. after a long night and welcomed into the world by both parents. Ironically, she didn't slow down the happy couple at all. They happily towed her about with them everywhere they went. Isa was a traveler from early on.

Later, with the arrival of Bailey, things became a little more complicated, but not by much. The happy family did everything together.

Chapter 32

What is it About Mexican Food?

"Here you go, you guys. I made peanut butter and banana. I put butter on the bread first like you like it, okay? I also made the oatmeal fruit bar. I used cranberry this time," Tom said as he handed Isa and Bailey their lunches before dropping them off at school.

He was off to the depot where the state vans were parked to see the mechanics getting them in shape, then to meet with Jim Baker for the latest in insurance complications. Jeez, if it wasn't one thing, it was another. It was like someone was intentionally throwing a wrench into this project. Two steps forward, one step back. But if this last step back wasn't resolved there would be no more steps forward.

He remembered the ancient stories of the gods in Olympus and how they entertained themselves looking down at humans, watching their struggles. To them, humans were entertainment, on which bets were cast and obstacles thrown in to see how they were handled. "There, let's burn down his house and see how he gets out of this one…haha," would be nothing more than watching a sporting event on TV for an Olympian god.

Tom sometimes felt like these might not be such fantastical myths. It seemed like the Universe derived entertainment from all his struggles. Otherwise, what was the point of having so much suffering and torment?

"Did you piss on the guy's cheese sandwich or what?" Patty barreled right through as he answered his cell phone on the second ring.

"Miss Patty! And how are we this morning?" Tom came back, trying to be cheery and bracing for whatever Patty was going to present, "… and what in the hell are you talking about?"

"Markowitz, the ADA. He seems to have a hard-on for you. What did you do to him?" She snapped back.

"I don't even know the guy. We've never crossed paths," Tom sputtered.

"I'm trying to tone him down, but I'm going to have to throw him something to appease him. He thinks you robbed the Tampa bank and probably Fort Knox, as well."

"I need to get a hold of Bartholomew, my accountant, and have him explain. But with the collapse of the company and everyone running for a new job, I lost him. Give me a few days and let me see what I can conjure up," Tom said.

"Aw'right, then. I'll do my best to keep Markowitz from blowing a gasket," she said and hung up.

Thank God, she's on my side, thought Tom. She was a bulldog and knew the law backward and forward. Hopefully, she could distract the DA long enough so they could get to the bottom of this mystery.

Later that afternoon, just after Tom picked up his kids, he was diverted to the arts and craft store to get supplies for school projects.

The obligatory stop at the new frozen yogurt shop lengthened the afternoon, but this was prime time to catch up with his kids and talk with them rather than to them. These moments are some of the little gems you remember while raising your kids. If you don't make the time, then you miss it altogether.

That evening, Tom met up with the girls at Cheryl's house for another get-together. He was so rushed after dropping off Isa and Bailey he didn't have time for dinner. Yet, on the car ride over with all the traffic, he remembered a chapter in a book he was reading last night, where the characters were having a fabulous Mexican dinner. The chapter described the special mole chicken with chocolate and chilis, pulled pork topped with cilantro and squeezed lime over a fresh corn tortilla; Tom started craving Mexican food.

"Tom wants to share with us some of his recent good fortune," Eve chimed in as they all started to sit around the coffee table in the cozy living room of Cheryl's Buena Vista house.

"Well, I think that's a little premature and generous of you to say," Tom said. "I may have landed a little state contract that a friend has orchestrated. It looks good, but there's a long way before the cash is in the bank."

"Oh, Tom, be positive. If you were presented the door of opportunity and you know you are capable, why shouldn't it come to fruition?" Anita pushed.

"I'm not trying to be negative, but sometimes it feels like a tease from the Universe," Tom replied. "I get thrown a tasty opportunity, but in the end, it's just out of reach. I'm not trying to be a Debbie Downer. I'm giving it all I've got to make it work, and I got a lot of good resources. Let's see what happens."

"Okay, let's meditate, focus on Tom's deal, and throw him some positive energy," Cheryl began.

"I'm in," Eve responded with a wink at Tom. "Maybe when he's rich and famous, he'll buy more herbs," she said with a smirk.

"Funny, Eve. I'll have you know I used my kids' ice cream money to buy the herbs the other day. I'm still trying to explain it to them. Thank God they're great kids, and forgave me," Tom added, feigning a bit of drama, putting his hand over his heart.

"Ok, you guys, enough bantering; let's focus," Anita interrupted.

The four were sitting in a loose circle and closed their eyes. They each began to calm their thoughts and focus on the NOW moment to center themselves.

Tom centered himself behind his eyelids and was focusing on observing the thoughts that flowed by from right to left, as he was a right-handed person, and escorted the thoughts swiftly past. The idea was not to get carried away with the incoming thought but to stay focused where you were in the NOW moment by simply observing them.

He began to feel—in the space, the texture, the expanse. He began feeling other presences in his space, and they were not toxic. They felt benign.

Through feeling, he wanted to incorporate these within himself, something his sense felt was the right thing to do. Sort of like the literal license in a dream where you see a character that was your third-grade teacher, but in the dream, it is a man, and your third-grade teacher was a woman, but in the dream it all makes sense.

They were strengthening him. It seemed the cumulative power of these other presences was making him stronger, although he did not know for what reason.

On a lull, the Mexican food from his book came to him. The vision of those delicacies flashed in images in his mind's eye. Although he imprinted them in his mind, he thought of them as a distraction.

After a while of holding on to this, he started to slip more often than not. Holding the focus position was sort of like an alcoholic talking himself into not having a drink. Tom needed to concentrate on every breath, "I am present..." and yet, he couldn't say it in his mind; he needed to just feel it. There were a lot of moving parts with this.

He finally came back to the present and opened his eyes. He looked around and saw everyone was also with their eyes open but had remained quiet — a reaffirmation of the quality of people around him.

"That was good," Tom finally broke the silence.

"Yeah, for me too," Eve added, along with Cheryl and Anita.

The evening had pushed along, and Tom saw the hour was getting late and didn't want to overstay his welcome at Cheryl's. He began to say his goodbyes.

Eve stood up after him and said, "I think I will leave as well, Cheryl, and get out of your hair. It was a great evening. Next time I'll bring some cookies and fruit." She turned to Tom, "I'll walk out with you if you don't mind."

They both left and were walking down Cheryl's front steps when Eve turned to Tom and said, "I'm starving. I missed lunch and dinner today. Do you want to get something to eat? My treat since you picked up the tab last time, and I had a couple of good sales today."

"Yeah, that sounds great. I wasn't thinking about it, but I haven't had anything since some toast for breakfast."

"Cool, then let's go. I have a craving for Mexican food, and I know this little dive a short-ways. Whaddya think?"

"Yum," he came back with a grin. "I was actually thinking of Mexican earlier."

Immediately after he said this, he wondered if his thoughts and cravings had spilled over to Eve. Could this be possible? Could his thoughts and feelings pushing out of himself have influenced Eve?

That would be too cool!

Chapter 33

Never Has a Rain Storm Not Cleared

"... so, I hadn't eaten all day, and I had this crazy urge for Mexican food, remembering this novel I was reading the night before. The characters meet at a Mexican restaurant, and the book starts going into elaborate detail about the different dishes they were having. I pushed this aside to clear my mind as I went into the meditation. Eve was there, along with the other girls. At the end of the evening, Eve wanted to eat Mexican. What do you think about that?" Tom asked Dora.

"Your Will is the most powerful force in the Universe," Dora began, "even the great master of Christianity said many times, 'with even the faith the size of a mustard seed, you can move mountains'. This wasn't just a cliché to uplift his followers, but Divine forces in action."

Tom changed his position on the chair.

"To... have command of your Will is the hardest endeavor you will have to face. These are the accomplishments of the masters, the enlightened. But it seems, Tom, that you may have scratched the surface on this." She looked at him with a quizzical expression like saying, *What do you think?*

Tom tilted his head with a *maybe* expression.

"One of the biggest frustrations people have when beginning their journey to meditation and these mysteries as they are called, although they are no mystery, but an inherent part of all of us, is that we don't know what we are looking for. How do the angels speak to us? Is it in English, Swahili, colors…? So, when something happens, you usually don't know it happened because you don't know what to expect."

"Tell me about it," Tom gently nodded in the affirmative, *makes sense*, he thought.

"Then something happens that you have a hard time distinguishing this reality from another. Something like your Mexican food implant into someone else's mind. Now, you can review or feel whatever you did to create the results."

His eyebrow raised with this understanding, *observe, observe, observe.*

After a brief pause, she continued, "Each of us feels things differently. What does chocolate taste like? For you, it is different than for me, but someone showed you a piece of chocolate and said, 'this is chocolate', and so you identify it as chocolate, although the taste and texture may vary slightly to me. Same with a color. The hue in a red may be different to you, but you now understand that we call this 'red'."

He stirred in his seat. Dora was delving deep.

"But with the mysteries, this is harder to translate to others. The gurus, the teachers, say, breathe in this way, breathe out that way, chant, look at a candle, and on and on. But each of us has to find our own way, not withstanding that there are basics like to calm and clear your mind." She went silent for another moment.

He reflected on his recent experiences with meditation. He nodded for her to continue.

"The darkness penetrates the weak of mind in this way. These forces gently worm thoughts and feelings into one until the person comes to understand these as their own thoughts and desires. Remember that. When you meditate and look within yourself, you know who you are and what is real. If you remove the desire inserted into the ego that sparks greed, fear, unbridled ambition at the cost of others' suffering, and even uncertainty, what remains, is the core, is the goodness of a man's soul." She paused to gather her thoughts once again.

"That would be the fire element. It is opposite with water. The line between love and hate is a matter of degrees, like cold and hot. Where does cold begin and hot end? If you have been skiing in the Rockies through the dead of winter where the temperatures are in the single digits, then sunbathing in a bikini or shorts on the snow during spring skiing season at 30 degrees is warm." She paused. "When you look back to where you have been, it's then you realize you were in the space all along. You just didn't recognize it," she was then silent.

It was a lot to take in. Nevertheless, Tom realized he must have tapped into something further that stirred Eve the previous night. They chatted for a little longer and talked about how he was doing with his projects, the kids, his ex-wife, and nothing in general.

"Well, Dora, I'll be getting along. Thanks for meeting with me," Tom said.

"Of course, darling. Call anytime, and don't get yourself all worked up. *Nunca ha llovido que no haya escampado*," she said, meaning, 'never has a rain storm not cleared'.

"I guess she was right," Tom thought. "Even the worst of them eventually blow themselves out," That, at least, was a comforting thought. "...and that goes for people, too," he chuckled to himself.

He needed to test this again.

Chapter 34

Rowing in Circles

"What's for lunch?" Bailey asked as he walked out of his room toward the dining area. It was 6:30 in the morning on a school day.

"You haven't even had breakfast, kiddo," Tom said.

"Yeah, but you make lunches fun," Isa hollered from her room.

"Did you make your bed? Then I might leak the information," he chuckled.

Tom had the kids several nights a week, and although he hated disrupting their lives, this was the best opportunity to enjoy them and grow up with them. These interactions are what made memories and for a meaningful life.

It hadn't always been like this, of course. Life with Ellie May had been a dream come true for a good while. Great and fun. She had been a real companion and friend.

When Isabella was born, it had been a magical era in their household. Although they both loved to travel and did even for short weekend getaways, Isa didn't seem to slow them down. They took her everywhere. Whether it was in a papoose or stroller, Isa was just another carry-on for them. They were a threesome, and they loved it.

Tom wasn't mega-rich by any means, but he had enough to be comfortable and travel a bit. One didn't need to be extravagant to enjoy the things that life brought them. Heck, even a trip to Key West by car was an outing. They would stay at an inexpensive motel near the pier, and the vacation was walking Duval Street and the pier when the cruise ships came in.

The pier was a party in and of itself. At the end of the day, they didn't spend that much cash. Sure, they could have stayed at the Ritz with the special ferry and drop $1,000 over the weekend. But their way was a fraction of that price, and they still did everything they wanted.

Bailey was born two years after Isa and was a welcome addition to the troupe. They were such great kids it was not a hardship to do more "staycations." Heck, they could still all go out together, it just wasn't as ambulant as before.

Little Bailey was quieter than the turbulent Isa, which made an interesting contrast. Tom thought often, *...they both came from the same parents, live in the same environment, and yet, are so different...*

He always so much enjoyed the interaction and tried to be a good example for them. Not that one can purposely "be" a good example. You are who you already are. Your children see this and absorb it from your actions.

We don't own our children. We are here as their guide, not to force our ways on them and try to mold them into what we think is the way to be. As Henry Higgins said, '...they have their own spark of Divine Fire.' We are here to nurture and fan that fire, Tom thought.

A bit of tension between him and Ellie May began when Tom started having money problems, and they had to hold back. When everything hit the fan with the Tampa bank, Ellie May threw in the towel. She apparently wanted more from life than struggling alongside Tom. And Tom supposed that was okay, we all want a better life, but sometimes one needs to steer like a sailboat. You need to go back to go forward or at least sideways.

The separation had been hard for both parents and children. But Tom was able to take the kids to school and pick them up as much as possible. They stayed overnight with him several times a week, so he was getting to see them quite a bit. Cooking for them and taking them to after-school activities strengthened the relationship even more.

Sometimes you abandon a ship only to find yourself rowing by yourself. It could be better to save what appears to be a sinking ship, as at least there are two or more rowers. Tom understood this wasn't always the case, and one didn't always know what the outcomes of any situation would bring.

"Yo, Tom," Patty greeted him when he answered his cell phone that morning. "We have a hearing next Thursday with the prosecutor and the judge."

"What the hell for?" Tom asked with surprise.

"I managed to arrange this before Markowitz goes to a grand jury and sets in motion something none of us wants. He's agreed to meet for an informal review. We can bring in witnesses, and they can as well. By the way, who is Campbell from the bank?"

Tom thought for a moment and responded, "That would be Anne Campbell. She was involved with government-related deals. She works out of the Tallahassee office for the bank, and she helped us on many occasions. I know Bartholomew, our accountant, was working with her recently. Why do you ask?"

"I'll let you know later."

They spoke a little longer and decided on a strategy for the following week.

Chapter 35

Cupcakes and Conundrums

The following few days were supposed to run smoothly, but of course, they did not.

Jim advised Tom that the insurance carriers wanted to double the quoted premium because the vehicles were owned by the State of Florida. This, apparently, opened the door for a greater lawsuit in the event one of his drivers had an accident. The additional premium bit substantially into the originally calculated profit margin, but the deal was already made, so Tom had to push through.

Jim was still trying to work it down, but he wasn't too hopeful.

"Dad, can you make twelve cupcakes for tomorrow, please?" Isa asked.

"What! Twelve cupcakes?" Tom was startled.

"Well, I gave some of my classmates a piece of the one you made the other day, and they said it was the best cupcake they ever had. So, I thought I could bring them some. But it's okay if you can't." Oh, she was slick alright, harping on her father's strings like a concert violinist.

"Ahh, sure, Isa. Let me check if we have all the ingredients, and I'll see what I can do," Tom sighed.

"Hi, Tom." it was Eve on the phone.

"Oh, hey," he answered, somewhat despondent.

"What's wrong? You sound like someone ran over your puppy," she came back, still cheery.

"It's just… you know… shit happening all over the place. Oh, I'm sorry. I don't mean to be a drip. Your call actually has cheered me up. What's up? What's happening with you?" He put on his best face.

"Well, actually, I wanted to invite you out," she said.

"Reeeaally?!" Tom said with a little playful sarcasm.

"Well, that's not fair. I did pay for the lunch last time. Didn't I?" she snapped back quickly.

"You're right. I stand corrected and, I might add, ungrateful. It won't happen again." They were having fun with their banter. "What or where's the invite?" He asked.

"Well, next week there is a fair at the Bayfront Park, and I will have an exhibit booth for the herb store. I wanted to see if you would like to come by. After the fair, we could have a picnic right there in front of the bay. How does that sound?" She was so upbeat.

"Well, Saturday, I have my kids, and I need to take Bailey to soccer, but that's at 7 a.m. Could I bring the kids?" He asked cautiously.

"Yes, of course!" She exclaimed enthusiastically. "That would be perfect because the whole thing is a family event, and there are tons of free rides and things for the kids… and I would love to meet your crew. I've heard so much about them from you," she said.

"Okay, then it's a date. What should I bring? The picnic? Let me know closer to the day," Tom said. "I know my guys are going to get excited about this… and Eve…"

"Yes?" She replied.

"Thanks, for real. You changed my day."

She could hear Tom's smile over the phone.

Later that day, Tom got a call from his mechanic, Felipe, who was in charge of the State of Florida's leased truck maintenance.

"Mr. Bennet," Felipe said when Tom answered his cell phone.

"Hey, Felipe. What's the word?" He asked.

"The word is not good. Half of these vehicles are on life support. I can keep them running, but it's going to be expensive. The one I am looking at now is going to need a transmission. What do you want me to do?"

Shoot me, thought Tom. *That would be a solution.* "Uh, Felipe, keep patching them up and let me see what we can work out. And thanks, I know you are a miracle worker. Just make sure none of these get stranded on a trip. That's one thing we can't afford, to have a truck break down on a delivery."

"Got it, nurse Nelly Nicam is on the way," chuckled Felipe, and they both hung up.

"Did I say two steps forward and one step back, or should I have said two steps back and one forward?" Tom said to himself. It seemed like every time something started to go right, he was slammed back down.

Chapter 36

It's a Beautiful Day for a Fair

Saturday finally arrived. Many people sleep in and relax, but if you're the parent of an eight-year-old, those days are not for you. Tom got up at 5 a.m. and made a light breakfast for his crew. He also had to prepare something for the picnic later that day.

Then, they were off to the soccer match, where Bailey happened to be one of the better scorers. There was a little click of three talented boys, and Bailey was one of them. Everybody had their chance. It's not like the three hogged the ball to themselves, but when there was an opening, and it was in their path, they took the ball.

It was a good match, and Bailey's team won so everyone was hyped up with enthusiasm. Afterward, instead of taking the kids for ice cream or some other treat, they were headed to the fair at Bayfront Park on the east side of downtown Miami on the edge of the bay. There, one can see the cruise ships and the inlet leading to the ocean, as well as Miami Beach and the different islands that spot Biscayne Bay. It's a beautiful park, and the city had done a nice job of revitalizing it several years back.

Tom parked some distance away and then took the elevated tram that loops around the city right to the park. It seemed less stressful than wondering if he had enough money in the parking meter and if his car was going to be there when he got back.

When they entered the park, there was a police station set up along with the park personnel. Tom, Isa, and Bailey were provided with a colored band with markings.

"You need to be together with your Daddy to leave the park," the ticket clerk spoke to the children, "Okay?"

They both nodded.

Then he looked at Tom and said, "The bands all match, so no one leaves the park without matching adult bands." He winked at Tom, assuring him they were on top of safety.

The kids, followed by Tom, then started to roam around and see if they could find Eve. Isa and Bailey didn't know what she looked like, of course, but they were on the lookout at all the vendor booths and stands.

The fair was spread out with a series of amusements surrounded by booths and tables. Finally, Tom spotted one that looked like an herb company and headed toward it.

"Do you have anything to make me smart and good-looking?" Tom asked the person whose back was turned while unpacking something.

Eve abruptly turned and started to laugh.

"I'm sorry, sir, there's nothing that can be done for you," she sputtered with laughter. Then she looked to his side and said, "Are these your gang members? They're adorable! Hello, I'm Eve."

"I'm sorry," said Tom, "where are my manners? Eve this is Isabella, known to her friends as Isa, and her brother-in-crime, Bailey. Guys this is Eve, my friend and a great tea maker as well."

Eve beamed at them and then looked at Tom and said, "There are a lot of free rides, but you can also buy a band and get on a bunch of others," she said. "The park has been sealed off and no child is allowed to leave without a band that matches their parents band. It's kind of neat."

"We know. We got the treatment at the door," everyone held up their arm to show their band.

Eve grinned. The crew was way ahead of her.

"Ahh, but I bet you don't have…" she rummaged around a little under the counter and then held up what she was looking for, "…these green bands. One for each of you," she said, handing one to each of the kids, "These are for the special rides. Each band is worth three!"

"Oh, so cooool," both kids exclaimed at the same time, "Thank you soooo much, miss Eve!"

There comes a time when one's children stand on their own and all the parental guidance and training is either there or it's not. When they come through for you, with even just the simplest courtesy like "thank you," and other gratitude you beam with joy. And so, it was with Tom when his kids responded to Eve, with not only an enthusiastic "thank you," but addressing her with respect for being an adult.

"Okay, you guys, go check out the scene, and I will catch up with you shortly. Let me help 'miss' Eve here unpack some things," Tom said, and the two ran off in a heartbeat.

"That's quite a cute set of people you're sport'n there, Mr. Tom," Eve elbowed him with a country twang while trying to hold back a laugh.

"Thanks. They do make me proud. They're just great kids, and it's not because they're mine. I mean it," he said as Eve was looking at him with an *Oh, really* look. "They listen, absorb my advice, and they end up making their own right choices. That makes parenting pretty easy. Not that they're perfect. They're still kids, and they do kid things like we all did, but, well, you know what I'm trying to say," he said with a pleading look that said *Don't bust my chops here, Eve.*

She smiled and nodded and thought, *This guy is something else in the way he interacts with his children*, and then said, "Tom, I'm seeing it. You don't have to sell me on them. My heart melted when they called me Miss Eve." She giggled at the thought.

A little while later, Tom caught up with Isa and Bailey who were standing at the entrance of one of the pay rides. "What's going on? Are you going in?" Tom asked.

"One of the rides charged Bai twice, and he doesn't have anything left on the band. I have the one left, and we didn't know what to do."

Tom could see Bailey was practically in tears. He looked over to the attendant at the gate of the ride and wondered how he was able to propel thoughts the other day at Cheryl's. He focused on the attendant and sent benevolent kindness to be open and generous toward others. He also sent calming his way.

Then, he bent down to eye level with Bailey and said, "Bai, go up there with your sister and tell the man you accidentally overcharged the band and ask him if he will let you accompany your sister on the ride."

"But Daddy, can't you do it?" Bailey asked

"I could, but it will be more powerful if it comes from you," Tom said to him. "Be brave and try. That's all we can do."

Little Bailey went up the ramp with his sister, and Tom witnessed the exchange from a distance. The next thing he saw was the attendant waving them through. Bailey turned toward his dad with a wide grin and shot his arm up to say, "Victory." It brought a lump to Tom's throat, not only for Bailey's success but for the fact that he did it all by himself.

There was also that little "thing" going on at the back of his head wondering how much his thoughts toward the attendant had influenced the moment. The occult works behind the scenes on what looks like everyday life.

Tom headed back to the booth to hang out with Eve.

Eve was talking with a potential customer who was describing some ailment. She had an intense, focused look with the customer and was nodding her head. She then looked back to one of her containers and pulled out a bag with herbs, doling out a measure for the man.

Eve proceeded to write down some instructions on how to administer the herbs, then said her goodbyes. The grateful customer waved and left with a happy and satisfied smile.

"That looked like it went well," said Tom.

"The poor man has been bombarded with big pharma medications, and he doesn't know if he is coming or going. I suggested he start with this mild tea mixture I combined, and maybe he can begin to ease off the more powerful stuff, with the consult of his doctor, of course. Long story short, with his cholesterol through the roof I suggested he may have developed an intolerance to animal fat and his body is no longer processing it, he should maybe try to go vegan," she said.

Tom looked at her sideways and said, "Vegan? Isn't that for the radicals and flower children?"

She looked at him like he just swallowed a baseball, "Tom, cattle can weigh up to 1,400 pounds, and they eat only grass. The silverback gorilla eats bananas, nuts, and grass. Horses eat grain and grass. All these creatures are more powerful than man. Yet, we eat their meat. How does that work?" She said. "The only creatures designed to process meat are probably the big cats. Don't get me wrong, I like a nice steak, but facts are facts, and we don't need to eat meat to get all our nutrition. Who knows if our degenerated old age, or rather, the condition we arrive at old age is derived from our lifelong diet choices?" Looking straight at him, she had an intense look that exuded her very concern for people's health.

"I never thought of that, but, yeah, cattle eat grass, and we eat them," he said. "But that means canceling ice cream, eggs, and a whole lot of things we eat and love if we go vegan." He was wide-eyed and incredulous.

"Don't shoot the messenger. I am just pointing out facts and observations. Do your own research and try to change your diet a little and see how you feel," she said. "Anyway, some people get to a point where they can't process animal fat. I have seen it before. They have to change their lifestyle. Like peanuts for some or shellfish for others. One day you wake up, and your body says, '*no mas*." She started to pack some things back in the boxes. "I think this is winding down. Why don't you go look for Isa and Bai, and I'll start picking this up?"

Tom saw Isa at the exit of one of the pay rides. "Isa, what are you doing? Where's Bailey?" He asked.

"He's finishing the ride," she said.

"What do you mean? How can you still have credits for rides?" Tom asked.

"We made friends with this girl. She had to leave and had an unlimited band, so she slipped it off without breaking it and gave it to us. So, I slid it on and go on any ride I want. When I come out, I slip it off and give it to Bai. We've done each ride like 50 times." She said it so nonchalantly, like it was the most normal thing to do.

Tom burst out laughing and shook his head. What a twist these two. When he stopped laughing, he said to Isa, "The fair is coming to an end. When Bailey finishes, head over to the booth, and we'll go from there to our picnic. Okay?"

"Sure, Dad," she replied.

Chapter 37

The Miracle of Life

Park security allowed Eve to keep her boxes of merchandise in a small, protected section so they could have their picnic.

They crossed over another section closer to the water's edge where they could enjoy the breeze and the view. They had downtown Miami on one side and Biscayne Bay on the other.

Tom brought a blanket, and some provisions including a nice bottle of *Pouilly-Fuissé*, one of his favorite light white wines. It had lost its chill, but according to Tom, this wine could be drunk in any fashion.

They were sitting on their blanket and just watching the scene. The families, the kids running around.

Eve gently placed her hand over Tom's on the blanket as they were both gazing out. Tom looked down and then looked over at her with a smile.

"What?!" Eve's silent expression read as if to say, "can't a girl show some affection?"

Tom gently nodded with a smile acknowledging the bond forming between them… and his genuine appreciation for another human being that cared enough and believed in him enough… something he had not experienced in a long while.

Tom looked over to his left, and there was a little girl, no more than three, and she was crouched, looking at a tiny flowering plant on the grass.

Tom just stared at her for a long time, and then a slight tear formed in his eye.

Eve was watching the water, but with Tom's silence, she looked over and wondered what was going on inside his head. She saw the tear and asked with genuine concern, "Tom, are you crying? Are you okay?"

"The little beautiful blank sheet of paper that is that little girl," he started, "has just noticed this little piece of creation on the grass next to her. She notices that one of the little flowers is still a bud, although she doesn't understand what that means. But next to it is the one that has opened and is blooming. The petals have yawned to an opening, and she sees the pistil in the center with its own little shapes and wings... and spectacular color at its center. Its perfection in symmetry. The color is vibrant and real, like the grass and her own hair. She doesn't yet understand these to be different than the paint on an automobile or the dye on her dress or some people's hair, but she's in awe of the magnificence. The magnificence of this simplicity right there in front of her on the grass. The awesomeness of creation in an ordinary setting has completely captivated her." Tom sighed and shook himself from his reverie. "I'm sorry, yeah. I was just looking at that little girl," he said.

Eve kept looking at Tom for a further explanation, but she said nothing while waiting for him.

"I just love looking at little people," he began. "They're such a clean sheet of paper. Everything to them is new and fresh. Their awe and wonder, that 'miracle of life', no, no, that miracle that 'is' life, is written all over their beautiful faces. It's just a wonder to see."

"But why are you crying?" Eve persisted.

"Because it's the wonder of life itself," Tom whispered back.

Chapter 38

Mira, Look What the Cat Dragged In

After Tom had taken the car to the designated repair shop so the city's insurance company could determine the damage and how much they were going to pay.

Sure enough, the city insurance was prepared to pay $2,300 to repair the damage to Tom's car after the garbage truck backed into it.

But Tom knew people; there was always "that guy" where you could get good work done for a little less.

Tom hoped his contact, Eduardo, would do the same repair; fix a couple of dings around the car and paint the whole thing.

"Eduardo, it's been a while," Tom said.

Eduardo, a stocky 5'9'', was behind a Chevy SUV with a wrangled left front fender. He looked up, *"¿Mira quien trae el viento?"* He said with a big smile spreading across his face as he looked up.

Tom spoke Spanish and new this to mean, "Look what the wind brings," similar in English to "Look what the cat dragged in." Tom replied with a grin, *"Las malas hondas,"* or "the bad waves," in English.

"What can I do for you, *amigo,*" Eduardo said as he grabbed Tom's arm with an affectionate embrace.

Tom had sent Eduardo's shop a lot of business over the years with his former company, and Eduardo was grateful for it. Eduardo was someone who did not forget his patrons or former patrons, no matter their present position in life. He was well aware of Tom's situation as the rumor mill in that industry was well-oiled. "Take a look at the car and let me know what you can do," Tom said.

Eduardo walked out to the lot and eyed the damage. After some time looking and measuring, he said, "Tom, the post was slightly damaged, but we can straighten that back. The door we can replace from a junkyard replacement. Of course, we do the paint here. Thirteen hundred, okay?" he said looking at Tom.

"It's okay. Can you do it now and take payment when the insurance company pays me?" Tom asked.

"Don't worry about it, Tom. When you have it, then pay me. You need to leave it for about a week. In the meantime, I can lend you that old Toyota over there if you need it," he said. Yeah, he knew Tom's financial situation.

"Yeah, that would be great. Thanks."

Humility is a hard pill to swallow when you have had means and now need a little help. Why not? Part of the reciprocity of being human is allowing yourself to receive. To let others give and let them have the satisfaction of being able to give as well.

"Thanks, Eduardo. I very much appreciate the loaner and helping me out like this," he said, trying to hold back the emotions and gratitude he was feeling.

They exchanged keys, and Tom headed for the old Toyota. When he reached his new ride, something he could not place tingled within him. He looked to his right, then his left, and seemed to be alone in the parking area.

Yet, there was that something happening in his chest area. He turned to look behind him, and that familiar vignette began to form in the center of his vision. It had the same foreboding feeling that rippled through him as before.

The temperature dropped. Then, coming into focus within the bastion of a flaming inferno was one very powerful arm holding a flaming ball.

Then, in the blink of an eye, the giant arm flung the flaming ball directly at Tom.

"DUCK!"

He heard someone scream, "Take this shit, asshole."

He turned and ducked just in time to have a bottle fly over his head and hit the wall behind him, shattering.

"What the hell was that?!" He shouted.

Eduardo ran out of the shop, "Oh my god, Mr. Tom, are you alright?" he said with exasperation. Then he looked around and saw the vagrant. "That asshole. I've told him to stay away from here a thousand times. I'll take care of him, but why don't you take the Toyota and go now." He looked at Tom as if to say, "It's best that your ilk not be in this part of town Kemosabe!"

"Got it," Tom said and scooted into the Toyota. It started right away, and he backed out and drove away at a sensible speed, but as quickly as he could.

As he was driving away, he couldn't help but think about the glass bottle that rocketed two inches from his head. Was this a coincidence? Or was this the dark forces pushing their way through… again? And what screamed in his head to "DUCK"?

He was beginning to get seriously pissed. Nothing was going to push him around or threaten him like that. He was getting an idea of how to counter this beast. He would need some help.

He would need the girls!

Chapter 39

The People Vs. Tom Bennet

The next morning, they met up at the courthouse steps for what was supposed to be an informal conference to review the possibility of moving forward with an indictment against Tom Bennet or not.

This was an unusual procedure as the District Attorney normally went in front of a grand jury and presented his findings, asking for an indictment. There was never opposing counsel, so the grand jury pool only got the District Attorney's presentation which made it practically a rubber stamp for the DA's request.

Patty had run interference. With her influence through the court system, she had created sufficient doubt that she was able to convince ADA Markowitz that it behooved him to discuss the matter before he could potentially make a fool of himself.

The matter was to be heard before Judge Marco James.

Tom spotted Patty speaking with a well-dressed gentleman, which Tom pegged as a fellow attorney on the courthouse steps. He made himself known but waited a few steps away so as not to barge in on their conversation.

Patty caught his eye and slightly nodded, acknowledging his presence.

After finishing her conversation, she made her way toward Tom, "How ya doin' this morning? Ready for combat?"

"I thought this was a friendly conversation? A preliminary discussion," Tom responded, a little confused.

"It may look friendly, but it's always adversarial with a DA that's trying to put you in jail, my friend. We need to head this off at the pass. He's bringing some witnesses. Ready?" She asked while turning and heading for the front door of the courthouse.

They went through the security clearance. Several guards acknowledged Patty with a nod and some comments about a case she had won. It was nice to see he was with an acknowledged veteran of the system, although he understood that guaranteed nothing.

They headed for the bank of elevators.

Stepping off the elevator on the 4th floor, they noticed a small commotion going on. It looked like a court decision was not going in favor of the defendant as there was a gathering around one man and what appeared to be his attorney. Either he was giving bad news, or they were strategizing on their next move.

Either way, it made Tom nervous; the affirmation that a day in court was always a crap shoot. No matter how prepared you thought you were, how much in the right you thought you were, something could happen that could come as a surprise.

They moved quickly to courtroom 4F. She walked in, and Tom followed. He looked about and saw that Eve, Cheryl, and Anita were seated in the general public section. He was a bit surprised, but he smiled and walked over to them. "What are you guys doing here?" He asked in a low voice with a conspiratorial tone. He had a "what the heck?" Look on his face.

Cheryl spoke first. "Eve said you might need some moral support."

"So, we rushed over," Anita chimed in. "But not before some chants and meditations last night."

Eve's eyebrows went up as if to say, "I have no control over these two."

"Well, thanks. Let's hope this goes smoothly," Tom said, and he moved to catch up with Patty, who had already arrived at the bar and was setting up her papers from her attaché on her table.

Markowitz had already arrived and was with a small team on his side of the room, conferring with each other. He seemed a bit smug, but that might have been Tom's opinion and not a fact.

Judge James entered the courtroom and sat at his podium, although this was not a formal trial nor even a hearing. It was a courtesy the judge was extending to provide arbitration and guidance in a non-committal manner. Markowitz could proceed to move forward with an indictment after the results from this meeting, but depending on what was presented, he could put himself on the wrong side of the court.

"Counselors, are you ready?" The judge looked back and forth between Patty and Markowitz.

"We are, Judge," they both responded in unison.

"Very well, Mr. Markowitz, please proceed," Judge James said.

ADA Markowitz stood at his table facing the judge and said, "Mr. Thomas Bennet, the possible defendant, has defrauded the First Financial Bank of Tampa and further attempted to extract more funds in some scheme. The people can present a bank witness available here today to testify to this. The People want restitution to the bank and jail time for Mr. Bennet for his misconduct." He proceeded to sit down.

The courtroom went silent.

Chapter 40

Benevolent Thought

Tom was still stunned, thinking that this wasn't just going to be a light hearing to clear up any misunderstanding. Slack-jawed, he looked over at Patty and heard her in *sotto voce*, "… that son of a bitch. So that's how he wants to play it?…" She looked over at Tom and faced him, "… let's play, then."

The judge looked over at Patty and said, "Counselor, are you ready?"

Patricia Amores, Esquire, looked over at Sydney Markowitz, U.S. District Court Assistant District Attorney, who was smirking like he had just blindsided her to make a winning move. Her look was not daggers, nor of shock (she was not going to give him that kind of satisfaction). It was completely neutral. She was an excellent poker player.

She stood and addressed the judge. "We are, your honor," she said in a clear, confident tone. "The government is trying to portray that my client, Mr. Bennet and his company, are involved in some high crime of thievery and fraud, but we can show that the bank is mistaken and has misread information in this case. There are other relevant facts, but we will await the esteemed Mr. Markowitz to present his case." As she finished speaking, she looked to her right while extending her arm toward Markowitz like a showman displaying his wares. She sat down. *Your move, baby*, she thought.

"Mr. Markowitz, you may proceed," the judge said.

Markowitz stood and walked to the center of the room. "In the year 2018, Mr. Bennet approached the First Financial of Tampa bank in Tampa, Florida, and proposed a need to expand his business. He applied for a line of credit for five million dollars, ostensibly to purchase inventory and working capital to go after some government business. The Bennet Company targets transportation work through trucking, small deliveries with vans, or even automobiles. Earlier this year, he applied for an additional extension of this line."

Tom and Patty were cautiously nodding watching the ADA

"However, when the First Financial of Tampa bank reviewed their client's bank accounts and the submitted financial statements, they were short two million dollars. Neither the accountant nor Mr. Bennet had an immediate response, and the bank had no alternative than to freeze the Bennet Company's bank account assets they controlled and cancel the line of credit."

Tom looked over to Patty gently shaking his head *it's not like that*, his expression stated. The girls in the back of the room, along with a few that had drifted in, were riveted to their seat.

"The government, on behalf of the bank, which is federally insured, is seeking repayment of the missing funds and looking to charge Mr. Bennet with criminal fraud on the theft. We have a representative from the bank outside this courtroom ready to testify on this matter." As he finished, a look of satisfaction was written across his face."

The judge nodded. "Proceed."

"The government calls Mr. Ephron Kimball," Markowitz said with a flourish as the rear doors of the courtroom opened, allowing Mr. Kimball to be let in.

Tom looked at Patty. He shook his head from side to side and sighed. Nothing further was spoken between them.

Mr. Kimball was guided to the witness stand and sworn in. Mr. Markowitz then approached him. "Good morning, Mr. Kimball. You have been sworn to tell the truth so we will expect your truthfulness as an officer of a federally insured institution."

"I am clear on my responsibilities, of course," Kimball responded.

"Please state your name, where you work, and in what capacity," Markowitz began.

"My name is Ephron Kimball, and I am the chief financial officer for the First Financial of Tampa bank. I also oversee the loan department."

"And do you know the person sitting at that table?" Markowitz asked, pointing to Tom.

"I met him for the first time at a conference meeting at our bank in Tampa about a month back. He was there on an application to extend the credit line the bank presently had with his company, the Bennet Company."

"Can you run through what occurred after Mr. Bennet asked for the credit line increase?" Markowitz asked. "Perhaps, what your bank did leading up to this meeting and what happened at the meeting."

"Sure," Kimball said, "Mr. Bennet approached us for an increase in his line of credit with the bank. As an existing customer, our procedure is slightly different as we already have the customer profile and the advantage of a track record of how he has paid his existing or previous obligations. We, therefore, reviewed his bank account balances and payment history, and submitted financial statements."

"Did you find anything irregular?" Asked Markowitz.

"We saw use in the credit line and then some consistent increase in usage with a very large drawdown recently. The financials did not reflect any increase in revenue, nor any corresponding offsetting asset to explain where the money went," Kimball stated.

"Did you pursue the inquiry?" Markowitz gently continued like an eight-year-old asking if Santa was real.

"We sent several messages to his accountant but received no reply, and then the meeting was upon us. We concluded there was misconduct underway and took action so as not to expose the bank any further," Kimball replied.

"So, knowing a fraud was being done to the bank," Markowitz started. "Objection, your honor," Patty leaped out of her seat.

"Counselor, this is a closed hearing. We will let the prosecution use whatever language they want. It is only us in the room, and you will have a chance for rebuttal," the judge responded, but one could see he was not pleased with the tone the prosecutor had taken.

"Continue, Mr. Markowitz," the judge said, facing the DA.

"Thank you, your honor, but I can rephrase a bit," then looking back to Kimball. "So, suspecting a fraud after your extensive review of the Bennet file, you shut down the credit line. Where are you now?"

"The bank accounts we froze had a total of $1.7 million," Kimball stated. "The $5 million credit line had been tapped for $3.87 million. So, to repay the bank, we are short $2.17 million."

"Did you ask Mr. Bennet where the money was?" Markowitz asked.

"Yes, but he said he needed to speak with his accountant. He has still not responded."

"So, if someone were to steal money from the bank in a manner to deplete a credit line with no intention to pay back, it would follow Mr. Bennet's actions?" Markowitz continued.

Patty jumped out of her seat, causing her chair to fall back behind her and clatter to the floor. All parties in the courtroom looked at her in surprise. She opened her mouth to speak, then realized the judge's admonition earlier. She gazed across the room at everyone looking at her, closed her mouth, shook her head slightly, and shrugged. She then turned around to pick up her chair, but the statement was made in the gesture. Markowitz understood he pushed beyond a professional inquiry... and it was noticed.

After the initial opening statement by the prosecutor, Tom had begun sending calming thoughts toward Markowitz to dissuade vicious aggression and to counter his career from taking a nosedive. He thought about the energy he had sent to Eve, moving her to want a Mexican dinner, and he directed the same to Markowitz. Heat is countered with cold.

He sensed that connection he had before with the girls. It seemed to strengthen him, and through a force of Will, he let out what he thought was a burst of benevolent thought focused directly toward Markowitz.

Pop! Clack!

Tom opened his eyes, and the sound directed him to the stenographer. She had her hands raised like the device had burned her fingertips. The look of surprise on her face said, "I've never seen *this* before!"

Everyone was now staring at her, including the judge. She looked back to the judge, "I'm sorry, your honor, I'm having some equipment trouble. I'll need to get a replacement device from my office."

Judge James looked about the room. "Let's take a recess for lunch," he said and brought his gavel down. The tension in the room had taken a new level, and the thump of the gavel seemed to break the spell.

Chapter 41

Tom Has Moral and Spiritual Support

After the judge left the chamber, Patty stood up, then looked over at Tom. "Let's get out of here and talk this over."

Tom stood, and as he looked back toward the door, he saw Cheryl and Anita and remembered the girls had come to show support. He walked back to them and asked, "Where's Eve? Wasn't she here with you?"

"She was," Anita began, "and all three of us were focusing our energies through you and on that prosecutor going after you. Then, all of a sudden, she was taken aback and said she needed to go out and get some air. We were going to accompany her, but this man's ravings kept us pinned to our seats. She should be right outside the door. Let's go find her."

Tom suspected what had happened but remained quiet on the matter. "Yeah, let's see if she's alright."

Patty had stopped to hear the conversation.

"Oh, sorry, this is my attorney, Patty Amores. Patty, Cheryl and Anita," Tom did the introductions.

"Yeah, she was terrific," Cheryl pushed in, "jumping down that guy's throat, but it seemed the judge had you choked back. I don't get it."

"It's just procedure," Patty said, "There is another side to this story. Don't worry; I'm going to get to tell it." Patty cracked a slight grin. "Let's go find your other friend."

They followed Patty out the courtroom door to the hallway.

They saw Eve a little further down sitting on a bench against the courtroom wall. She had a water bottle in her hand, and her head and back were against the wall as she looked up.

Tom rushed forward and sat next to Eve, "Eve, honey, what happened in there? You're pale."

"I don't know. All three of us were trying to join our energy, like we did the other night, and try to quell that maniac's attack on you. My god, he was making you out like the next Bernie Madoff. Tell me you didn't do all those things, Tom?" She was pale and showing signs of fatigue.

"Of course not. That's how he wants to present his show. We still have ours to present."

"Well, anyway, we were connecting. I felt it, and I know Cheryl and Anita did too. Then, something overcame me. It, like, took my breath away. Something from within. I got scared, Tom. I'm not afraid to tell you. I can't explain it. It wasn't a feeling, nor any kind of vision. I guess I could say it was a 'knowing' that something bad would happen to me if I didn't stop right then and there." She was staring at Tom with wide eyes, and yet, it was like she was not seeing Tom but beyond him, remembering the event.

She was on this side of terror.

"Okay, let's meet tonight at Cheryl's house. I have to confer with Patty during this lunch break. Perhaps you should go home," Tom said.

"No, we're all staying for the afternoon session. We're with you, Tom. Front and center." Her composure was coming back with all the determination she could muster.

There's something to say for women with gumption. They can break your balls, but they can also carry the day for you. Eve was one of them, along with Cheryl and Anita, of course, but Tom was clearly developing feelings for Eve. He had denied it to himself before, but her actions and determination on his behalf now made it difficult to ignore.

Patty had been on the phone all this time in view, but not on top of them. Tom met her eyes as she was finishing up, and she jerked her head to one side, indicating, "let's go." He moved over to her. Patty closed the call and with a sly grin, said, "We found him; let's go to lunch."

Chapter 42

Lunchtime Strategy

"Who's 'him'?" Tom finally asked as they sat down at a café a little way away from the court crowd.

"'Him', is your former accountant who disappeared on you when the shit hit the fan, if I may remind you," she said with a note of satisfaction.

"No friggin way?!" Tom shot back in a low voice as he leaned in toward Patty. "Where?"

"He was back in his home country, Jamaica. His father was very sick. On his deathbed, I think. When the bank froze your bank accounts and you abruptly closed operations, he didn't see a need to stay and flew back to Jamaica," she went on.

They conferred further on what tactic she had in mind. "Of course, things can change once we get underway. I need to be nimble on my feet when the show starts," she said. "By the way, what was that all about with those three ladies? What are they talking about 'sending energy his way', and things like that? Are we so desperate we need voodoo or something?"

"You don't need to be a cynic, Patty," Tom said, half in jest. "There are forces greater than us and with some care and believe we can…" he paused. "We may… be able to sway them in our direction for more favorable results," he said, lightly touching the topic.

"I know, I know. Keep your shirt on. I'm not a cynic. It's just that results don't just happen. You have to make them happen. In this world, action makes things happen—as you know, coming from being a once successful businessman. Hopefully, you'll get back there one day so you can pay my fee for getting your titties out of this ringer." She was just so unorthodox you had to love her.

He let out his breath, not realizing how much tension he was storing in the low conversation. He leaned back in his chair. He looked at Patty and had to laugh. She was tough as nails, but her tender side had no bounds.

The waitress arrived with lunch. They had ordered light as neither was very hungry after the attacks during the morning session.

In the back of his mind, but not that far back, Tom wondered about the girls and Eve, in particular. If their efforts were so "innocuous," then why had Eve had this, shall we call it, "incident?" Were they stirring up forces that bite back? Yeah, results didn't just happen, as Patty noted, but someone was always moved by something. A thought, a feeling, an intuition. And where did those come from? Who made those "happen?"

Chapter 43

Kimball is Back on the Stand

During the lunch recess, after meeting with Patty, Tom conferred with the girls and compared notes on the meditation and focus tactics he had experienced earlier. They concurred that they, too, were focusing benevolent thoughts and could very well have enhanced Tom's. They agreed to continue their efforts with the bank witness and Markowitz, focusing on calming and non-combative thoughts to counter any greedy, self-serving thoughts these two could have at the expense of others.

After lunch, Patty recalled Ephron Kimball of the First Financial Tampa Bank back on the stand.

"Mr. Kimball, these are informal proceedings, but please remember you are still under oath to tell the truth. Are we good there?" She asked.

"Yes, of course," Kimball replied.

"Can you refresh us on the relationship between the Bennet Company and First Financial Bank of Tampa and why it started?" She began as nice as could be, like a curious bystander asking if the ice cream sundae came with nuts.

"As I mentioned before, Bennet applied to our bank for funding to help him win some government contract," Kimball began.

"You did not," Patty interrupted.

Kimball looked up with a perplexed look.

"You did not mention Mr. Bennet had applied because of a government contract," Patty clarified, adding the "Mr." to Tom Bennet's name to humanize her client, rather than the perceived liability for the bank.

"All right then," Kimball replied with what appeared to be a little testiness in his tone. Patty could see this senior bank officer was not used to being challenged or corrected.

"Please proceed, sir," Patty gently pressed when Kimball hesitated, perhaps regrouping his thoughts.

"He applied for the loan, and everything checked out. Regarding his credit and the financials, we reviewed bank balances from his other bank accounts and the government contract he was being considered for. The application was taken to the loan committee and was approved."

"Were there any issues with the approval? That is, were any members of the loan committee in objection for any reason?" Patty asked.

"No, not that I recall. I think it was unanimous as everything fell into place, as I just mentioned," Kimball said.

"Was the credit line used? How was it maintained? That is, how were payments made on it?" Patty asked.

"The line was used and paid down multiple times. Payments were made on time, monthly. There was never an issue with us," Kimball stated.

"So, when the Bennet Company requested additional credit for another government contract, it did not raise any red flags. Would that be correct?" Patty asked.

"Objection, leading witness," Markowitz shot up.

"Counselor, as I mentioned to Ms. Amores earlier, this isn't a trial. It is an inquiry. Furthermore, you were given a wide latitude, which I may add you took advantage of. We are going to give Ms. Amores the same courtesy." Then after a slight pause, "Proceed, counselor," Judge James said, looking at Patty.

She nodded. "You may answer the question, Mr. Kimball," the judge said after turning to look at Kimball.

"No, the additional request was not unusual, but the short fuse and pressure to get the approval very quickly was," Kimball said. "We practically had to have a special loan committee convene for this."

"Did the rush request trigger anything special from your office?" Patty asked as she turned to face Kimball.

"Any time someone is in a hurry, it is a red flag for us," Kimball replied.

"Even though the request was clearly for an awarded government contract, of which copy was part of the loan application package?" Patty added with an incredulous tone.

"Well… yes. We want to be thorough." Kimball was now showing a little nervousness that the bank may have unfairly targeted this customer. "But that is how we found the discrepancies," he finished a little too satisfied with himself.

"And what exactly were those discrepancies, Mr. Kimball?" Patty was now pressing. Not accusatory, because she still was behind the eight ball, but planting the seed of "maybe the bank was creating a situation that just didn't exist."

"Uhmm, I can't think of any at the moment," Kimball responded, trying to put a brave face where there was no basis for the bank's behavior.

There was a pause; she turned, looking at her table, then abruptly turned back to the witness, "Does the bank offer any other service aside from loans?" Patty continued now that she had softened Kimball a little and taken his superiority down a few notches.

"Well, yes, the bank has estate planning and consulting services for stock portfolios. It also can manage and trade stocks." Kimbell welcomed the opportunity to get off the other track.

"Does the bank offer a service for assisting or consulting on working with government contracts?" Patty shyly introduced the question.

"Uhmm, I think there is something, but I am not sure… maybe, compliance?… I am not sure. I don't deal in that area," Kimball said.

"So, if Mr. Bennet was working with another department in the bank that dealt with government contracts, you would not know about it?" Patty asked.

"It should be in the general customer profile, but that profile is separated into various segments. Loans are in one segment. If you have a stock portfolio, it is in another segment, and so on and so forth," he blurted out, trying to show these things were not of his concern.

"Would reviewing the customer profile be part of your loan inquiry?" Patty cautiously asked in a neutral tone so as not to sway Kimball either way and not to cause suspicion.

"We do a cursory look, but we are more concerned with the financials and the customer's ability to repay the loan to the bank," Kimball responded.

"Who is Anne Campbell, Mr. Kimball?" Patty then asked after a slight pause.

"I don't know," Kimball replied, wondering if this was a trick question.

"Would it surprise you to know Anne Campbell works for First Financial of Tampa Bank in the government consulting office?" Patty asked.

"A lot of people I don't know work for the bank. I'm not in human resources," Kimball shot back, somewhat smug.

Patty turned from the witness stand and walked back to her table. She picked up some papers on her desk and turned around, facing the judge and witness.

"I have here an affidavit from Anne Campbell stating she was working with Thomas Bennet and the Bennet Company for a specific government contract. She is unable to go into further details on the nature of the contract for security reasons, but she does clarify the Bennet Company was required to place $2,350,000.00 in an escrow account with the government's name on the account as surety for placing the bid." She had her hand up in the air holding the documents like a paperboy peddling his newspapers.

"I quote, Anne Campbell – Tampa Bank – 'an account was created for a DOD contract, that's the Department of Defense, that required the Bennet Company to fund the account as a deposit for the work to be done. The account had the DOD agency name on it with Bennet as a signatory. It did not show up as a Bennet Bank account'," she added.

She looked back to Kimball, "That's where your missing money is, Mr. Kimball."

Chapter 44

Patty's Surprise Revelation

Judge James slammed down his gavel repeatedly to calm the courtroom after Patty's last declaration.

Markowitz had jumped out of his seat and was chomping at the bit to speak with Kimball. He waited for the courtroom to settle.

"Judge, I had no idea…" he fumbled to get the words out.

"You'll have your opportunity, Mr. Markowitz," Judge James retorted.

"Mr. Kimball, did you ask the Bennet Company for an explanation of the missing money?" Patty continued.

"We reached out to the accountant, but did not get an answer and since this was a rush, we thought we were getting ambushed," Kimball said defensively.

"And you didn't think to look at the customer's profile to see if there was something else there?"

"The profile isn't a place where we could expect to find missing funds." Kimball was now trying to justify the bank's clear oversight.

"And, yet, it was, wasn't it?" Patty finished for him. She didn't wait for a response and reached over to her desk, and with a raised hand holding up a piece of paper, said, "I have here an email from one Mr. Frederick Bartholomew, accountant for the Bennet Company. He is presently in Jamaica. He went back to his home country, Jamaica, when he learned his father was very sick. On his death bed. He notes he may have not added the surety deposit notation on the financials as it was not in the Bennet Company name any longer, and the contract had not been awarded. It should have been on an explanatory note, but he apologizes for not making it clear. With his father's illness, he was not thinking clearly, he says.

Nevertheless, he states the notation was in the financials and should have been clear to anyone that reads financial statements." She turned to Kimball, "Mr. Kimball, did you personally review this file?"

"No, I have a team of analysts do that leg work. They then summarize the file and make recommendations."

"It appears like a breakdown in bank procedures, what with the failure to review the customer profile, which would have alerted the Bennet Company involvement with a government contract and, more importantly, with the bank's consulting service. It appears the financials were not adequately reviewed as well, causing a misconception as to the financial position of Bennet and its cash position. And all these... *failures* on the bank's behalf caused Bennet to lose the government contract and have to close his business."

"Objection, your honor," Markowitz jumped up. "Please, your honor, the counselor is taking this too far," he pleaded. He was hemorrhaging and was begging for a lifeline from the judge.

Patty looked at the judge, "I'm finished here, your honor." She headed back to her table.

The judge turned to Markowitz. "Your turn to cross-examine—if you wish, Mr. Markowitz."

Markowitz was already standing and moved quickly to the witness stand, "Mr. Kimball, is there anything you did differently with the Bennet Company file than you would do with any other customer file?"

"No," he was about to add something else but closed his mouth instead.

"How was it possible to misinterpret the financials as counsel just mentioned?" Markowitz was trying to throw a softball question. Few were available.

"The Bennet Company financials are very complex. They have governmental requirements, deferred income, deferred liabilities, and now this escrow for bids in play but not consummated. I think anyone could have missed this. Add to the fact the accountant did not follow up and respond for clarification, and you have a situation like this." He would not go as far as to say, "a mistake." He would not put the bank in liability... no matter how ugly the situation against the bank looked.

"Thank you, Mr. Kimball," Markowitz filled in with a sigh of relief, taking advantage of the momentum for the retort.

"The government rests its case, your honor," Markowitz turned to sit at his table.

Tom looked over to Patty. She was stoic, "It's not over till he throws in the towel or the judge discourages him from proceeding," she said in low voice out of the side of her mouth.

Tom nodded and had the focus firmly in his mind, although now with his eyes open.

"Mr. Markowitz," the judge looked at him and paused while he stood, "do you still want to pursue this in light of today's... ahh,.... revelations?" He posed the question.

Markowitz was conferring with Kimball, who was now seated with him at the prosecution table. "I think we are going to table this while we confirm all the details brought to light today, your honor," he said.

The proceedings were adjourned.

Chapter 45

Otherworldly Repercussions

They walked out of the courtroom and met the girls in the hallway. Eve was pale and a little dazed.

Patty turned to Tom, "Meet me at the coffee shop in, like fifteen. I need to talk to a few people first," and she walked off.

Tom turned to Cheryl, "She doesn't look much better." Then turning to Eve, he asked, "How are you feeling? You don't look so good."

"A little nauseous," she said. "It started when we were building our energy toward the prosecutor and the bank guy, what's his name. I was feeling fine, and it seemed like I had a handle on my focus, then… I don't know… it felt like it came back at me. I don't know how to describe it. It came back in a negative way. We were pushing out positive, benevolent thoughts and bad, bad waves came back at me."

He looked down at Eve's hand, which he was holding. "What are these lesions on your arm, Eve?" He asked with astonishment. Cheryl and Anita leaned over to take a look as well. They each looked at each other with an "I've never seen this before" expression. "And something is forming on your neck as well, Eve! What the hell is happening here?" Tom stammered in a menacing tone. He didn't know where or to whom to direct his venom.

"We were concerned," Anita added. "We didn't know if she stressed herself, depleting her own lifeforce, or if she stepped on the wrong toes... spiritually speaking, that is."

"I'm thinking along the same lines," Tom said. "Listen, ladies, I need to confer with Patty, but let's meet at your house later and talk this over."

He left the girls after a few more minutes trying to console them and headed to meet Patty at the coffee shop they agreed on.

When he reached the coffee shop on the corner, it was after the lunch crowd and not overly full. There was what looked like an attorney speaking with his client, an elderly couple, and two retiree guys over in the corner.

He decided to take a seat at a table near the two retirees, uninterested in having to overhear private legal conversations.

The waitress came by and dropped off the menu. "Would you like something to drink to get started?"

"A coffee would be fine, and I am waiting for someone else. Thank you."

She went to start his order.

"... the flanking maneuver was used by Hannibal in the Battle of Cannae. He may have been the first; I don't remember," the first retiree was saying.

"... you mean when the attacking army is duped to approach, and once in the killing zone is attacked on both sides by the opposing force?" The second retiree replied. "Awww, it was used many times, Sam. Why the Greeks used it in the Battle of Marathon. Hell, even Stonewall Jackson used it on the Potomac in the Battle of Charlottesville. It's so classic, and the other side always gets caught off guard." He was almost cackling.

The two were old veterans chewing the fat over military strategy and history. *Some days you just need to kick it around,* thought Tom.

"Hey, Mrs. Kravitz, mind your own business." Tom nearly fell off his chair as Patty stood over him grabbing the other chair. She had entered the shop, and Tom was so entranced with the retirees' conversation he had not noticed.

He chuckled, "Yeah, I know. These guys are exchanging war stories and save the world strategies," he said. "They're actually quite knowledgeable. I was about to join in," he jabbed sarcastically. "Okay, enough of that, explain to me what I just saw," he said, leaning in with his elbows on the table.

Patty adjusted herself in the chair and leaned in so as not to be overheard. "I spoke with my source at the DA's office; we definitely halted their attack. It's not over, and we may not get an official 'it's over' response from them. Also, I was speaking with an associate, and we may be in a position to sue the bank for negligence and causing you to lose the government contract and close your company. Whether it's successful or not it will throw them off their game. Since no indictment was filed, there isn't much cause against the DA's office, but Markowitz definitely has egg on his face for not investigating this further before beginning this escapade," she leaned back. "We did good today, but let's not rest on our laurels and I'll research the countersuit option and let you know."

"So, we live to fight another day," he said as he leaned back as well. An enormous pressure had been lifted, although there were many other battles. "You know I'm tight for cash, but I can send you, like $500 and send more for later."

"Send it. I can at least buy myself a pot pie," she said with a grin.

She is sort of like a hard-boiled egg, Tom thought, *hard on the outside, but soft and tender on the inside*. He smiled and nodded in appreciation.

They said their goodbyes and went their separate ways. Tom needed to get his kids from school, and he would just have enough time with the afternoon traffic building up. He hoped he could drop them off at their mom's house as he needed to head back to his home office and catch up with some emails and calls. He wouldn't mind taking a 15-minute nap as he was exhausted from the day's events.

Isa and Bailey's pick-up, mercifully, did not involve any sports practice drop-off, but they did need to go to the arts and craft store to get supplies for a project. Of course, Tom had to hold back random purchases they kept throwing in the cart as cash was not in ready supply. That hurt him tremendously, as he would love to buy his kids whatever they wanted, but he just couldn't. Ten dollars here, twenty-three there... it added up faster than it was coming in.

They had a soft pretzel from the stand outside the arts and craft store and sat on a nearby bench, chomping on their snack while they talked about their day at school.

After a little while, he dropped them off at their mother's house and headed back to his own. When he arrived, he was going to go to his computer, but instead, he went to his bed and lay down. He closed his eyes for a second and was instantly asleep.

Chapter 46

An Uneasy Dream

He was in a space. It was neither pitch black nor was it light. It was more like dusk where you have visibility up to a certain distance, and then it becomes too difficult to see much further. You know there is a beyond, you know the distance goes on and on, but you can't see it.

The space felt neutral. That is, he felt neither malice nor benevolence in the space, but he was tranquil. Around the periphery, he started to notice plants, then trees. He was in a clearing in a jungle.

Observing his surroundings, he began to get the feeling he was not alone in the jungle anymore. Something malevolent was approaching. Then he saw it straight in front of him at the edge of the clearing, slowly breaking out of the foliage.

He instantly became alert. He couldn't see clearly what was at the opposite end from where he was standing, but it was big. It moved like a cat, cautiously, but purposefully and directly toward him.

He was uneasy and with growing fear, yet there was still calm. An assurance within him that, in spite of these horrific odds, he could still be in control and dominate the situation. He had it within himself to overtake this threat.

He was getting butterflies in his chest area. This cat-like thing with yellow orbs for eyes was looking directly at him and ever so slowly moving toward him. It was inevitable where this was going.

The spacious jungle around him seemed to be closing in on him; all he could do was focus on this creature slowly approaching. It was almost like he had tunnel vision. It was frightening, yet intoxicating. Sort of like the desire to ride a roller coaster; you want to be scared out of your wits, but you really don't.

The creature had stopped. It was not moving closer but cautiously observing.

Then it occurred to him to pull, to bring the creature to him, to lure it. He remembered that mean dogs are attracted by your fear. *I guess all bullies are*, he thought.

So, he conjured up a feeling within himself of being frightened. The smell of fear on Tom lured the big cat closer. And closer still.

It didn't growl. It didn't even make a noise. It was completely silent. If Tom hadn't seen it, he wouldn't know it was there, nor coming toward him.

The cat was now directly in front of him. Its amber eyes were now looking directly at him and somehow changing in demeanor. Where before they were searching and smelling, now they've found their prey.

The eyes turned menacing as they peered into his soul. Then, another change incompatible with animal behavior came. Those eyes turned to hate.

There was a startling painful growl, and the cat leaped directly at him....

Tom sat up from his bed, gasping. He was perspiring. His hands were wet, as was his neck. His pillow was soaked.

He turned and sat at the edge of his bed with his feet on the ground, catching his breath as his heartbeat began to come down.

He staggered out of bed and changed into some casual clothes, then made a calming herbal tea for himself. *An Eve tea*, he thought with a smile.

He headed to Cheryl's house without further delay.

Chapter 47

A Confrontation at Cheryl's

He arrived at Cheryl's a little after seven. There was still some light outside, and incredibly, he found a parking spot quickly near the front of the house. His parking angel was on duty tonight.

He walked up the steps, and before knocking on the door, it opened. Cheryl was just standing there with concern, her head tilted, indicating "head on into the living room... stat."

Tom nodded at Cheryl and entered the house.

In the living room, Eve was on the sofa sprawled out with one leg hanging onto the floor. She was not looking too good. Her skin was pale and grey.

Tom absorbed the whole scene and turned to Cheryl and Anita. They conferred for a few minutes and went back to the living room.

Tom kneeled in front of Eve and held her hand. "Eve," he whispered.

Eve blinked open her eyes. "Hmmm," she said as she focused her gaze on Tom.

"Eve," he started, but the words would not come out. From embarrassment? He didn't know.

"I can't even begin to repay for what you've done for me," he muttered. "No one has so unselfishly thrown themselves in such a treacherous path on my behalf." His eyes were beginning to water as he looked down on her physically beaten body.

He was waddling in a little pity party, but quickly snapped out of it. Seeing Eve like this imbued him with even more strength and determination. He was getting more pissed by the minute. No *one*, no *thing* was going to take her away from him, no matter where it came from! He shook her out of her reverie...

"We are going to try something, and I need you to be as brave as you have been for me all day and muster your energy and focus with us. Are you okay with that?" He asked.

"Yeah, yeah, I'm still here. I'm good. Just tell me what to do," she said, a little groggy.

Just then, Cheryl entered the room with a tray of mugs filled with Tulsi tea, "This is the Queen of Herbs, folks. It should prepare us with a calming of our souls," she chuckled, trying to sound sarcastic to lighten the moment, but in actuality, she was perfectly serious. They needed all the help they could get, and she knew it.

They all sat around the coffee table with lit candles at its center. Eve sat up on the sofa with Anita at her side. Cheryl was on a chair to the side, and Tom was in a chair opposite her. More candles were scattered around the room providing ambient light. The room lights were turned off. Together they formed a semi-circle.

Cheryl lit an incense stick and placed it in the incense holder on the coffee table. The incense was more to clear the air and create an atmosphere of focus on one specific theme... the Self.

They sat with their eyes closed in silence, and Cheryl set the tone by starting a repetitive chant in a low voice. After a few minutes, she stopped, letting the last of her chant vibrate off into the far expanses of the universe.

When his thoughts began to calm, and he was in the Now moment, Tom became aware of his surroundings. The space was wide and deep.

There was a sense about it that it was living and a part of him, that he belonged in it. If he were to try to explain in words, it wouldn't make any sense as the space was all about him, and yet within him at the same moment.

He was one with it.

From the edge of his periphery, Tom sensed a darkness, like a blotch of ink, but it was still. Like when prey captures its victim and lays on it either to claim it or gather its thoughts on how to devour it.

Then the thought entered his mind to purposely attract this malicious, dark force. He didn't understand why he would want that but was compelled to do it anyway. How, though?

The idea that he should feel fear would create an excellent target for a dark force to attack. Darkness preys on the weak and dependent.

With a volition of pure Will, he began to generate a sense of fear in his chest area. It felt like butterflies before public speaking, and it started to expand to his outer limbs.

He was so concentrated on the change in his body he didn't notice a change in his surroundings. The space around him seemed to be getting colder and darker. It was closing in on him like a small room where the walls feel like they're getting closer and closer. His breathing started to get erratic, and the fear he generated began to grow stronger, further attracting the force now overtaking him.

He started shrinking back on himself as the darkness kept moving toward him. It was getting closer and starting to gather onto itself, getting thicker and denser with each passing moment.

When the darkness was centered in front of him and very close, he smiled.

He raised his hand high in the air like a symphony conductor and just as quickly from all three sides, right, left, and behind the darkness from where it came, a brilliant light shone on the concentrated darkness in front of him.

A shriek of an ungodly nature shattered the air around it, yet the brilliant light continued unabated.

The brilliant light, which felt more powerful than the sun, was now penetrating the ball of concentrated darkness. Through the piercing light, he saw the image of a Satanical-looking being—a horned creature, with fanged teeth and red in color. He was screaming in agony as his flesh was sizzling off him, smoking in his destruction. "Yooouuu…" its accusatory eyes on Tom. "AHHH," the creature hissed and screeched like fingernails on a chalkboard. It was sizzling and disintegrating under the light.

Suddenly, from the left of Tom's vision, an energy emerged and flung what appeared to be a lance of energy toward the Satanical creature in front of him. It sliced clean through its neck in a sizzling spectacle.

Another shriek, and with its arms flailing, the creature pointed its right arm in the direction of the lance and spurt out a stream of heat energy that looked and felt like a flame thrower.

The energy image fell back, but the Satanical creature vaporized with its partially severed head.

Tom sat up from his chair, gasping. He was perspiring. His hands were wet as was his neck; his shirt was even soaked.

Everyone in the room was now fully alert, including Eve.

He knew what just happened. This wasn't a "what the hell happened to me?" Moment. Nah, not this time.

Tom knew what they had just done. He looked at everyone in the room. Stunned, he let out a long breath he didn't know he was holding in. He blurted out, "humph." Then, another and another until he started to laugh out loud. The girls joined in a release of unexplainable tension that had been permeating them since Eve had taken ill at the courthouse.

The room wasn't in shambles, but they all were.

They looked at each other, and Tom said, "Do I think we did what I think we just did?"

Eve was the first to respond, "You better believe it, baby, because that shit is off of me." She was laughing in a joyous tone like when an underdog athlete comes up victorious. You can't believe you pulled it off, yet the undisputable facts are in… and you are giddy… there is just no other word for it.

"Well, we did this together. No doubt about it. A 'Pincer Maneuver' I overheard earlier today. Isn't that some coincidence, huuhhh?" He said out loud, almost to himself. He was also in a daze.

"There are no coincidences, Tom," Anita said. "You overheard what you were supposed to." She grinned with a "think about it" look.

In all their celebration, Anita noticed Cheryl was joyous but not moving from her chair. She looked closer and shouted, "Oh my god, Cheryl, what happened to your arm?!"

Cheryl's arm was badly lacerated and still bleeding. "I got my licks into the bastard," she coughed as she put her head back, exhausted.

Anita and Eve jumped over to her to make sure she was alright. She was. They gave her a little water, cleaned her wound, and opened the windows for some fresh air.

Eve had a glow that looked like it was coming from the inside and shining outward… if that was even possible. What was real was that she looked great! Even her lacerations were looking better.

Tom was plastered with his back on the armchair. He looked like he had run two marathons, and he felt it. "Ah, girls, it's been real, but I gotta get outta here," he said. "Don't take any offense, but I need to leave this space. I have to clear my head. "What just happened here…" he started to say but trailed off.

"… is something quite profound, Tom," Eve finished.

He nodded, still speechless. Then he stumbled to get up and wobbled a little. Eve rushed over to prop him up as he found his balance with her help.

They walked to the door together. "You want me to go with you?" Eve asked with genuine concern.

"No… thanks, Eve. I really appreciate the gesture, but I need to be alone for a little and sort this out. I feel like we have penetrated a new frontier… like they say on *Star Trek*. And I'm not sure how to boldly go." He was gently laughing to himself.

"*Vaya con Dios,*" she said and stood on her tippy toes to kiss him on the cheek.

He was taken with her sincere compassion, and his eyes glistened as he took in her presence. Before he could make a fool of himself, he was able to barely push out a "Thank you" and then hurried out the door.

Chapter 48

A Final Visit from Messenger

Tom was exhausted. He headed for his favorite bench at the beach park.

The tranquil scene at the park at this time of the evening, the gentle lapping of the water, and the view of the expanse of the bay; it was like a balm for his psyche.

He needed to review what had just happened. No, what he had just done. Better yet, what they all had just done.

Clearly, the event had happened because Eve was now well. Whatever "cloud" had been over her was now gone, and it happened after the session. This was not in anyone's imagination. It actually happened in real time.

"Am I interrupting something important?" a voice to his left asked. It was a woman dressed in an ordinary dress from an overstock store. "… was going to rest my bones here."

"Yes, be my guest," he said as he slid over to give the lady more space.

They both looked out over the park and the water in silence for a few minutes, then the newcomer said,

"You had quite a night, eh?"

It took Tom a minute to absorb what was going on. He then looked over at the lady beside him. "You're the messenger," he said as a matter of fact.

"Yeah, I thought I'd switch it up a bit. Last time I left you here, I had some ladies trying to hit up on me, and I didn't want the hassle," Messenger replied.

"That's hard to believe because you were ugly as shit," Tom jabbed, just like Messenger jabbed at him.

"Cute," he said. "You've been challenged quite a bit. That's not to say everyone else isn't. Really, everyone is throughout their lives, and many times, but yours has been especially interesting. The way you've handled it is attention-getting."

"What do you mean?" Tom asked.

"Your challenges weren't that exceptional," he began, Tom looking over at him with a raised eyebrow. "What, do you think you're the first person to crash and burn financially? To lose his company and become broke overnight? Pleeezzz!" She scoffed.

That's 'cause you didn't lose it, Pal... Tom's expression said.

"Your persistence on this material plane, and then the attack on the Spiritual side is what is eye catching —that shows a level of your understanding of the nature of the Universe and where you fit in it. You seemed to be stuck on our first encounter, but this is why the darker forces wanted to stop you.

Tom nodded reviewing his experiences.

"You've penetrated a cloud that overshadows many people's ability to see clearly... of clarity. The dark forces are afraid because you are showing others this path, and they wish to keep them under their dark cloud of confusion and fear. They want to keep manipulating them with greed, aloneness, and the sense of separateness and guilt. Your showing others ruins this, and that is why they want to take you out."

Was that a compliment?

"You caught them red-handed, as they say. Bravo! But the battle is not over. As long as you breathe on this earth, you will be challenged. But as the great master of Christianity said to Satan when he was tempted with all the riches they were observing from the mountain overlook, 'Begone Satan,' and he was left alone ... at least for a while."

Tom was beginning to feel he was not alone, but was in the footsteps of greatness before him.

"Knowing where it comes from and why is more than half the battle. But not all challenges come from the dark side, my friend. Often, we misinterpret what we call adversity with guidance from the Divine Universe. A father prohibits his child from playing video games, perhaps during the school week. Is he punishing his child or guiding him to do well in his scholastics so the child can achieve to be a doctor or scientist?"

Tom thought of his own Isa and Baily and smiled.

"If a door is closed to you, look for the one that is opening... because there always is one. Perhaps, the Divine understands you were going in a direction that does not lead to where YOU want to go. Something YOU chose of your free Will. Looking at things in this manner will lead you to be more grateful for what is presented to you." She paused.

There was silence for a few minutes while they looked out over the tranquil scene. Tom was absorbing everything Messenger was saying. Then Tom shuffled in his seat and began to speak as if he were pondering aloud, "I'm hearing what you're saying, and I want to believe it, but I have worked like a dog all my life to build what I had. I was careful with my marriage and children, and where am I? I'm living in a borrowed bungalow out of pity from the owner. I'm broke and in debt. My car is presently smashed. I have the IRS after me and perhaps the Department of Justice too. My life is pretty shitty right now," he finished.

"Really?" Messenger responded in what initially sounded like a genuine tone, but underneath there was a bit of sarcasm. "Hmmm. Do you mind if I review with you?" Messenger said in a way one's mother would say to check how you cleaned up your room… knowing you were going to catch hell.

Even as a woman, Messenger is an asshole, Tom thought shaking his head. "Yes, go ahead, please, by all means," he responded with a sense of resignation.

"Many years ago, you had prayed that what you wanted most was to be able to enjoy your children. Sitting on the back of your palatial home on the veranda, having breakfast with them before they went off to school. Does that ring a bell?" She said.

Tom reluctantly nodded.

"I believe I see you taking them and picking them up from school every day and so you *do* enjoy seeing and doing with them. You *are* a part of their lives, interacting with them. Wasn't this your number one priority wish? Yes?"

"Yes," Tom replied a little reluctantly with a quizzical expression, his head turned away a little. Yes, she was right, but it was not how he had envisioned it. But he did have what he wanted with his kids. Furthermore, his work now, or lack of it, allowed him to take them and pick them up from school, something he would never have been able to do running the Bennet Company. He could even go to lacrosse and soccer games at four in the afternoon. Damn, the bitch was right.

"Let's talk about the company you built," she continued, "It was a good company, and your efforts were true and sincere. What I mean by this is you built it stone by stone. There was no treachery or underhanded maneuver that put you on top. I got that. The successful company and all its trappings began to distract you from the things *you* truly wanted in this life. Yes?" she nodded.

"You're not here to build a company. Your journey is for greater things. They may seem less great to you now than a big impresario of a powerful company, but helping a struggling waitress, alerting a young woman on sickness building in her stomach, giving guidance and being there for your children—these things have meaning. Heroes are everyday people. They don't wear capes, but they're heroes to those whose lives they touched because they did their genuine best with the resources they have. Maybe it was just a reset, and you will build a bigger and greater company, but now with this new knowledge. Look at all that has happened because of the company issue. Look at the good things, the things you have wanted in your life, that are flourishing because the burden of the company is no longer on you."

"Nothing happens without good reason, and everything that happens to you happens for a purpose… and at the right time. I know in your heart you already know this, but it's good to hear it again. Hearken to your spirit and let it guide you, for it is your true Self."

She paused for silence and then continued, "You know all this. Everyone knows all this. I'm not telling anything that you don't already know. But with all the white noise you experience in this life, sometimes you need a reset to remind you of your dreams when you were 16 or 18 years old. Those were true, those were real, but sometimes, in this very busy and complicated world, we get lost and accept the path of least resistance. Satan has a strong hand in this."

Tom took a deep breath.

"You're bummed out about the marriage. Let's talk about that," she plowed on. "When you married, you had an airplane, a nice house, a successful company, and an attractive material lifestyle. Is this what you were offering? Was the marriage built on this material base or on your genuine persona? I know this hurts Tom, and I'm not judging or giving an opinion. Only you, in your own heart, can review this."

This was the first time the Messenger had called him by name. Tom was taken aback because, for the first time, there was some compassion, even sympathy in Messenger's tone.

"Of course, when these things ended, what was left? If you stop making your rent payment or car payment that will end your housing and transportation. Yes?" She said sincerely, like a teacher trying to get her prized pupil to understand an important concept. "Now you have nothing except yourself to offer as a companion. Isn't this what *you* wanted? A relationship with another for no other reason than to be with the genuine self of the other?"

She paused again, if not for effect, then to let Tom take a breath. The Messenger knew she was coming at him fast and furiously. After a short silence she continued, "Eventually you realize that Santa Claus doesn't exist," she paused, "… as initially described. Oh, he exists, but he comes from the spirit side to you and all men. He sweeps in and brings out in people kindness toward others, giving, sharing from the bounty we have received, even those that have not received material bounty… as we conceive it… give of their time to the less fortunate, bake from their kitchen, or some craft."

"Oh, Santa exists, all right."

"Sometimes the Angel comes to you. But sometimes you are the Angel… moved by the Hand of God. Let yourself be open to this. Listen to your inner voice, your inner feeling. This is your true Self."

"… and your very first wish?"

"So, it appears to me, although I'm no one to opine on anything, that your balance sheet is pretty heavy on the positive side. That is, if you consider the things you have wanted in your life. Granted, it hasn't been served up like you thought, but if you look, it's been served well," she slipped in.

She stood and without further comment or goodbyes, walked off.

Epilogue

She was sitting on a low-ride beach chair under the shade of a palm tree overlooking the sandy beach and the water's edge. Her feet were extended, toes buried in the sand.

"So, Tom, whatever happened to that IRS audit and the charges?" Eve asked as she looked over to Tom laying on a wide beach towel.

He leaned up on his elbow and turned to her.

"Well, as things turn out, there is a little-known item in the Internal Revenue Code called Offer in Compromise, where they allow you to make a deal to repay the debt. I had to send in all my financials, and copy of the last three months' bank statements which, coincidentally, shows that I'm broke," he began, then added, "Lucky you, huh? Hanging out with some broke guy with kids and other baggage."

She smirked. "Go on, Mr. Bojangles; you can always dance for food," she giggled.

He laughed. "So, they offered me a deal of $12,300 to pay off the whole thing."

"Noooo waaay,...and what are you going to do? Where is the money coming from?" She asked.

"Well, as it happens, the state contract includes an up-front stipend of $23,000 to get the trucks in shape to operate," he said. "I'm going to use some of that money. Felipe, my mechanic angel, says he can work with that for a little while and stretch some of the maintenance, but we will need to get the work done sooner than later. The cash flow will start coming in within the month. It'll be tight, but it will work out, and I'll have the IRS off my back."

"Slick," she said, nodding her head in approval. "I'd ask you to help me with my taxes, but since you almost landed in jail on your first filing, maybe not." Now she was really laughing.

"Cute, very cute," he retorted.

They were silent for a few minutes, enjoying the tranquil view of the surf and people in the water, kids jumping up and down. She then turned to him. "What happened at Cheryl's…" she cautiously began. "What are you going to do with that? Where is that going… do you think?"

He leaned back up on his elbow and looked out over the water. "A long time ago, I wanted to look out over my veranda at my fortunes. Then, I realized how hollow it was, and I asked for more… to understand the mysteries of our being… or at least more; perhaps to be an active participant in the positive movement of this world we live in," he paused, reflecting a bit, then turned to Eve. "I have been shown, I think, that may be a bit pompous. That is, to be rolling in dough, *and* be some High Priest," he chuckled. "… to even aspire to be such an adept. But I want to think there is an in-between. After all, this is a very bountiful Universe, and the Divine can be most generous," he said with a sly grin.

"I need to make money, and there is no sin in living a comfortable life, but I am pursuing the development of my 'gifts'," he emphasized this last word, "for positive means." He paused again, "… as I may be guided to do … by higher forces."

They were both silent for a while. Then she looked straight at him and said, "Take me with you."

He nodded.

They both looked out at the serene waters, and after a while, she asked, "So, what happens now with this Markowitz and the Department of Justice thing?"

"Patty thinks it will wither away. The prosecutor and the DA's office in general got egg on their face by not doing due diligence on the accusation from the First Financial of Tampa Bank. She thinks I should go after the bank for defamation and loss of revenue caused by their actions. I'm not sure what to do yet. I think I'm going to let sleeping dogs lay."

"That's a relief," she said.

"Quite" Tom added.

She was looking over at Isa and Bailey playing at the water's edge and having a grand old time, "… so how are Isa and Bailey fairing through all your adventures?" She asked. "Do we see a psychiatrist in our future?" she was grinning knowing these two kids were about as normal as you could get, and Tom's attention to them had a big part in it.

He exhaled while laughing gently. "These two never cease to amaze me. You're right to say they should be psycho kids, and I know you're joking. After all they've been through, they could easily be bitter and bratty, police at my doorstep, kicked out of school,…yet they aren't," he said. "I'm just the luckiest parent alive," he was smiling at her. "We were talking the other day, and she tells me she's a happy kid. I couldn't believe it, I would've probably been bitter that I had been shortchanged by life, but here…" he was shaking his head, smiling with his eyebrows up in a look of disbelief.

"I'm amazed how you take this so 'in stride'," she added.

"You don't need the parachute until you jump out of the plane. The Universe sends you what you want… what you need, when you need it. What is the point of getting the great airline ticket deal if you can't use it? When you are ready to travel, the good ticket deal comes," he said.

"But what I mean…" she was starting to say when Tom's cell phone rang.

He picked up the phone and punched the answer key. "Hello."

"Is this Thomas Bennet?" The caller started.

Oh, here we go, thought Tom, "Speaking, how can I help you?"

"Mr. Bennet, my name to Major Charles Atkinson with the U.S. Army procurement team out of the Charlotte office. Lieutenant Anderson with the Florida Department of Transportation provided me your contact information. We have a situation where we need transportation logistics similar, if not larger than that agency. We're in a little bit of a bind because we are approaching the end of our fiscal year. Our budget is mostly depleted, but we do need the work done, and there is little time to do this through the bid process. We are able to approve a contract on a justified basis if we can get a good number from the vendor. Anderson said you worked very flexible with him."

Tom had already sat up on his towel. Eve was staring at him, curious as to what got his attention.

"I'm very flexible, as Lieutenant Anderson mentioned. Can you give me some details of what we have to work with?" Tom asked.

"At a minimum we need twenty trucks, but it could build to fifty. We can pay $1.06 per mile and we will guarantee 50,000 miles per year per truck. This could be higher, and probably will, but this would be the contractual guarantee," Atkinson said.

Tom's mental calculator was already on high gear—50,000 x 1.06 = 53,000 x 20 = $1,060,000.00 per year and that was the minimum guaranteed. Yesssss!

"What about the trucks?" Tom asked.

"You will need to procure these. We pay for deliveries at the stated sums," he said.

"What about any inflation provision, fuel price increase; that sort of thing?" Tom asked.

"Our standard contract for this type of logistic work would be for shipments along the eastern corridor. Anything west of Georgia and the Carolinas would get additional pay per mile. Anything west of the Mississippi gets an additional tariff per mile. We can add a provision for fuel surcharges and other inflationary costs. What did you have in mind?" Atkinson asked.

"Well, let's say we'll absorb any increase up to, say 10%, but if the environmentalists go crazy and it goes higher, then you guys would need to kick in some kind of fuel surcharge and the cost of tires. That sort of thing. Does that sound reasonable?" Tom asked.

"Yeah, I think we could live with that," he came back. "What do you think you can do?"

"Well, I'm interested, but let me check my resources. Can I get back to you later? It is the weekend," he said as politely as possible.

"Of course, and I apologize for the call on a Saturday. We were trying to catch up. I appreciate that you took the call and I will wait to hear from you. Thanks again." He hung up.

Eve was staring at him, speechless.

"What, I can't get a business call on a Saturday?" Tom asked with a mock defensive look on his face.

"What the heck was that about?" Eve asked. "You had such an intense look and it seemed like the wheels in your head were grinding so fast smoke was coming out," she said with a grin, happy to see Tom back in the game.

"A deal, believe or not, coming to *me*, this time, without the groveling. But, and I don't want to sound ungrateful, these things always seem to happen when I can't do it." As he was finishing his sentence, his cell phone rang again. "What the hell is goin' on, for god's sake? It's still Saturday, isn't it?"

He answered his cell phone. "Hello, Mr. Bennet?" Came a cheery voice at the other end. "Tim Benitez. I'm Mike Alvarez's boss from Trucking Logistics. I hate to bother you on a Saturday, but I was catching up to see if you thought about the truck fleet Mike talked about?" He sounded both hopeful and a little desperate.

Tom was silent for a moment; his wheels were in over-drive.

"Tim," he finally came back with a 'what will it take to get you off the phone' tone. "How many vehicles are we talking about that you want to unload?" He let "unload" drop, implying Trucking Logistics was in a bind and needed to move these vehicles, and he knew it.

Benitez took the bait and was ready to accommodate. "We have 28 on the lot ready to go now. As Mike mentioned, you have great credit with us from all our years together."

He waited with a long, pregnant pause for effect, then said, "I could be interested. I would need a lease arrangement with no initial payment—18 cents per mile, and I will guarantee 50,000 miles a year. I want a six-month moratorium on payments. I'll take all 28 trucks."

The phone line was silent.

"I think we can accommodate that," Benitez finally came back. "When should I draw up the paperwork?" He asked somewhere between being squeezed and grateful for the deal.

"Next week, I'll be ready. Can I call you at this number?" Tom was looking at his caller ID.

"Yeah, I'll look forward to your call. And thanks," Benitez said and then disconnected the line.

Eve was looking at him like a commodities trader in action, "Wow, you're quite the mover and shaker." She kidded him but with a look of wonder and admiration. "What was that all about, if you don't mind my asking? It's just that you were so intense, like a fox chasing a rabbit. You're quite the negotiator there." Her face had a startled look.

"Life," he said.

The End

...or is it the beginning?

Acknowledgement

Dear reader, I hope you enjoyed the story and most important gathered some tidbits that can work for your daily life. I have freely extended the use of some occult powers, but do not be misled, not by much. What our protagonist, Tom manages is within all of us. I hope you believe and accept this as true.

I want to acknowledge and thank several people. I'll keep it short. A story like this starts as an idea in one's head. I want to thank my cousins Ulisses and Henry for making me put ink to paper. Also, Amelia Pierce and the great team at The Reading Glass Books for their patience with the publishing aspect, Joshua Rivedal for the editing, and those little comments that make a sentence so much more. My sister Mayi and brother Frank for their continued support

"Witty, well written, funny, sad; it shows how resilience can get you through the darkest periods in your life and, the value of friends and family coming together and supporting you to make what you thought was your downfall into a lifealtering detour for a better life." —Ms. S, AMAZON Customer Review

"Wow! What a great and fun read. It was fast paced. I couldn't put it down. Funny and yet moving at times with wonderful points of wisdom and reflection. Something we can all use at times. Loved it!" —Margarita B, AMAZON Customer Review

"A wonderful debut novel. Sharp, witty dialogue with a ring of personal experience. An overall enjoyable read that leaves you with an encouraging outlook on life."—Luis Santeiro, AMAZON Customer Review